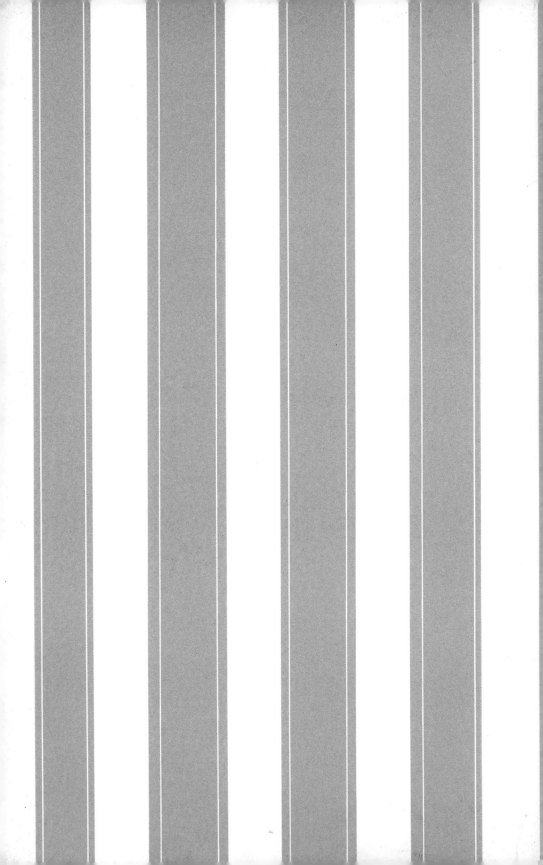

Strawberry Shortcake™

Return of the Purple Pieman

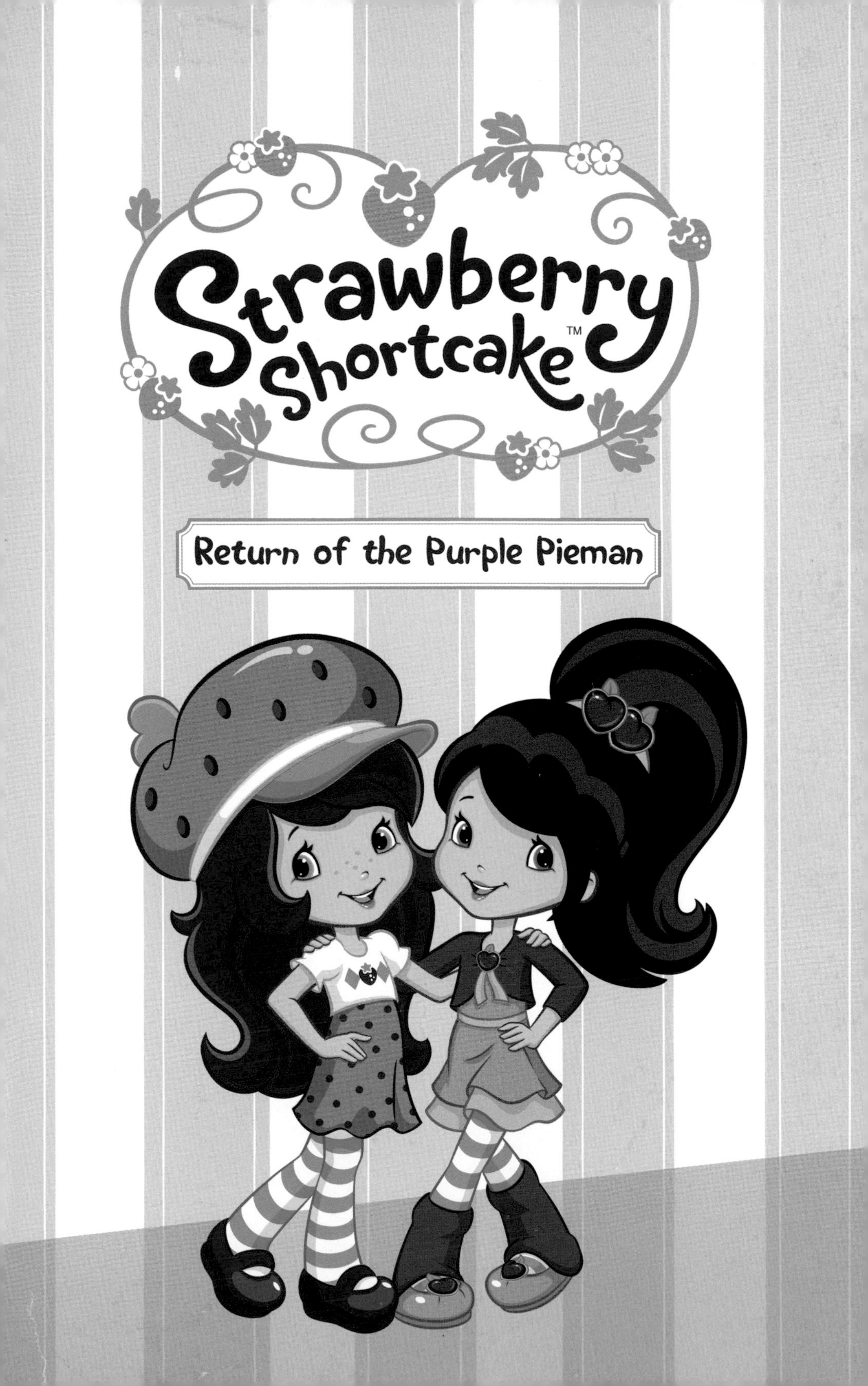

Strawberry Shortcake ™

Return of the Purple Pieman

Become our fan on Facebook **facebook.com/idwpublishing**
Follow us on Twitter **@idwpublishing**
Subscribe to us on YouTube **youtube.com/idwpublishing**
See what's new on Tumblr **tumblr.idwpublishing.com**
Check us out on Instagram **instagram.com/idwpublishing**

www.IDWPUBLISHING.com

Ted Adams, CEO & Publisher
Greg Goldstein, President & COO
Robbie Robbins, EVP/Sr. Graphic Artist
Chris Ryall, Chief Creative Officer/Editor-in-Chief
Matthew Ruzicka, CPA, Chief Financial Officer
Dirk Wood, VP of Marketing
Lorelei Bunjes, VP of Digital Services
Jeff Webber, VP of Licensing, Digital and Subsidiary Rights
Jerry Bennington, VP of New Product Development

ISBN: 978-1-63140-712-3   19 18 17 16   1 2 3 4

Originally published as STRAWBERRY SHORTCAKE issues #1–2 and STRAWBERRY SHORTCAKE FREE COMIC BOOK DAY EDITION.

For international rights, contact licensing@idwpublishing.com

Written by
Georgia Ball

Art by
Amy Mebberson

Colors by
Amy Mebberson
and **Fernando Peniche**

Letters by
Robbie Robbins

Series Edits by
David Hedgecock

Cover Art by
Amy Mebberson

Collection Design by
Claudia Chong

Collection Edits by
Justin Eisinger
and **Alonzo Simon**

Publisher
Ted Adams

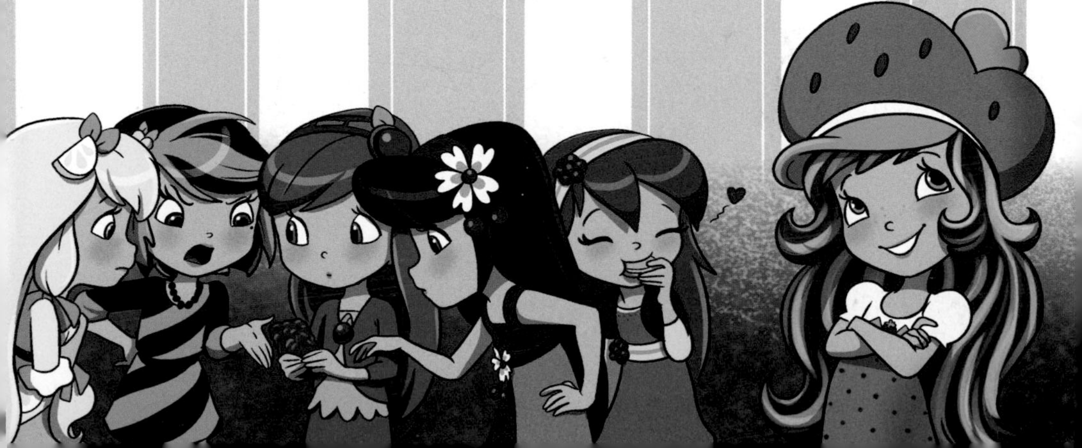

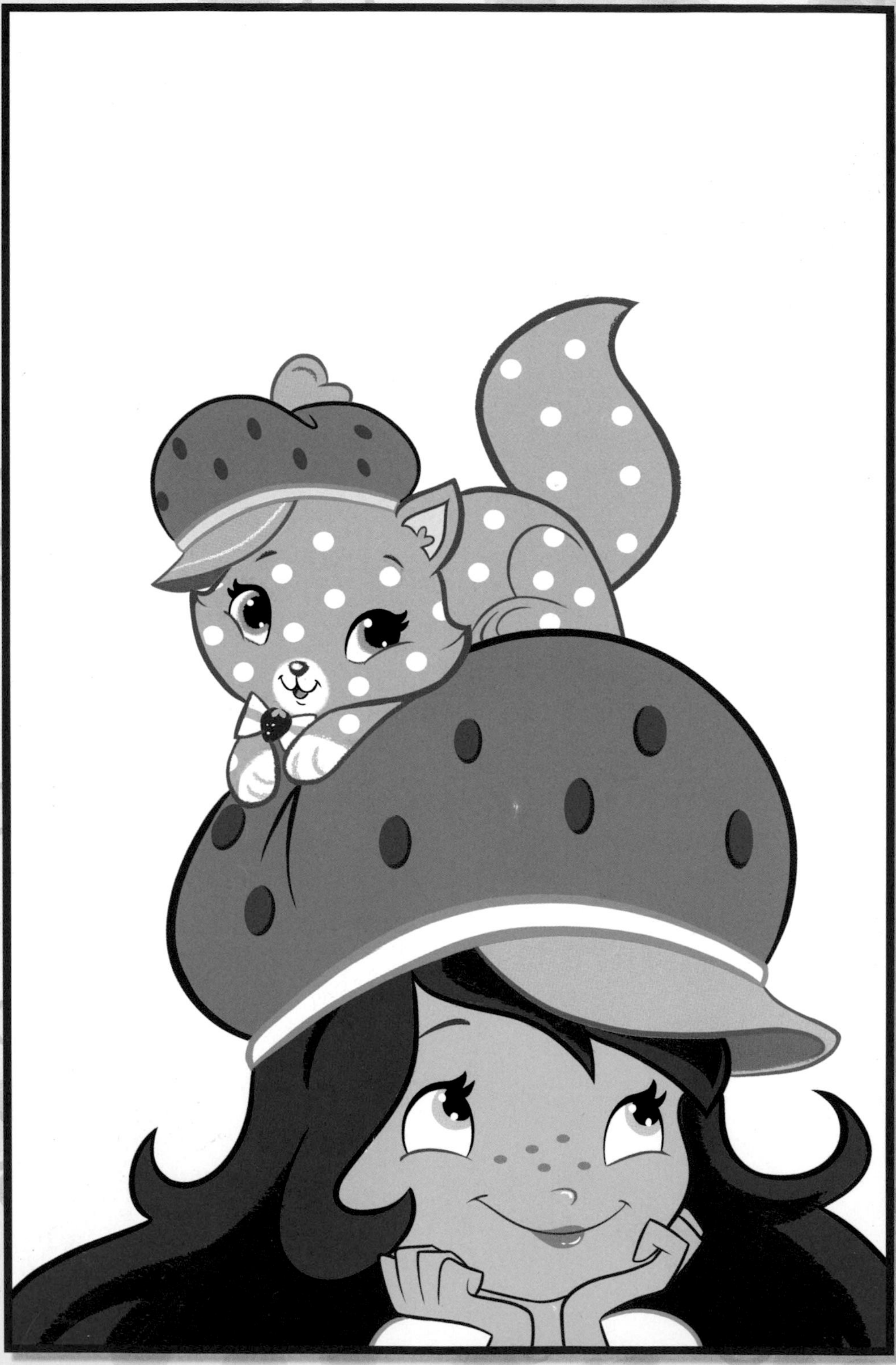

COVER ART BY
Nicoletta Baldari

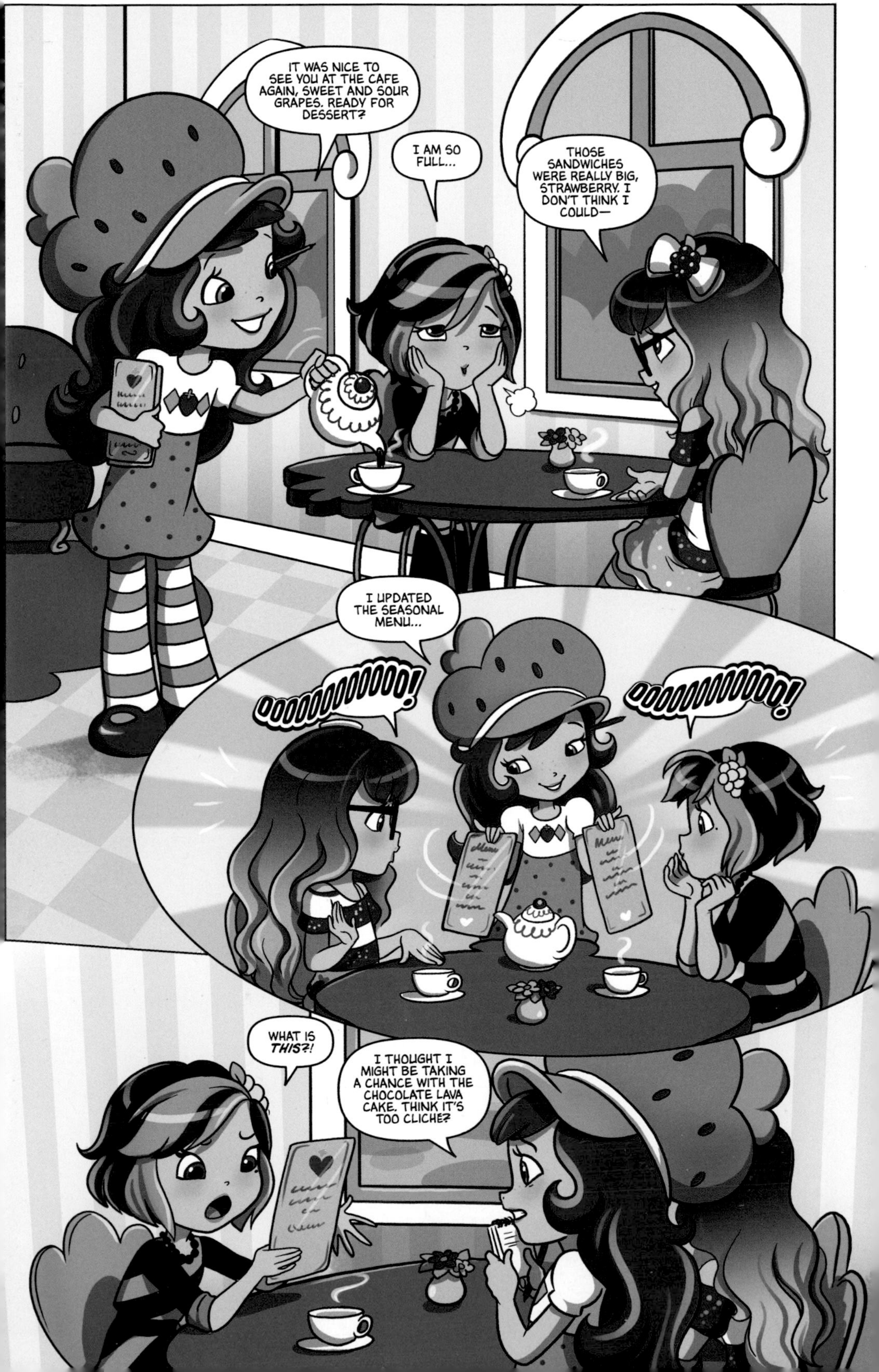
IT WAS NICE TO SEE YOU AT THE CAFE AGAIN, SWEET AND SOUR GRAPES. READY FOR DESSERT?
I AM SO FULL...
THOSE SANDWICHES WERE REALLY BIG, STRAWBERRY. I DON'T THINK I COULD—
I UPDATED THE SEASONAL MENU...
OOOOOOOOOOOO!
OOOOOOOOOOOO!
WHAT IS *THIS*?!
I THOUGHT I MIGHT BE TAKING A CHANCE WITH THE CHOCOLATE LAVA CAKE. THINK IT'S TOO CLICHE?

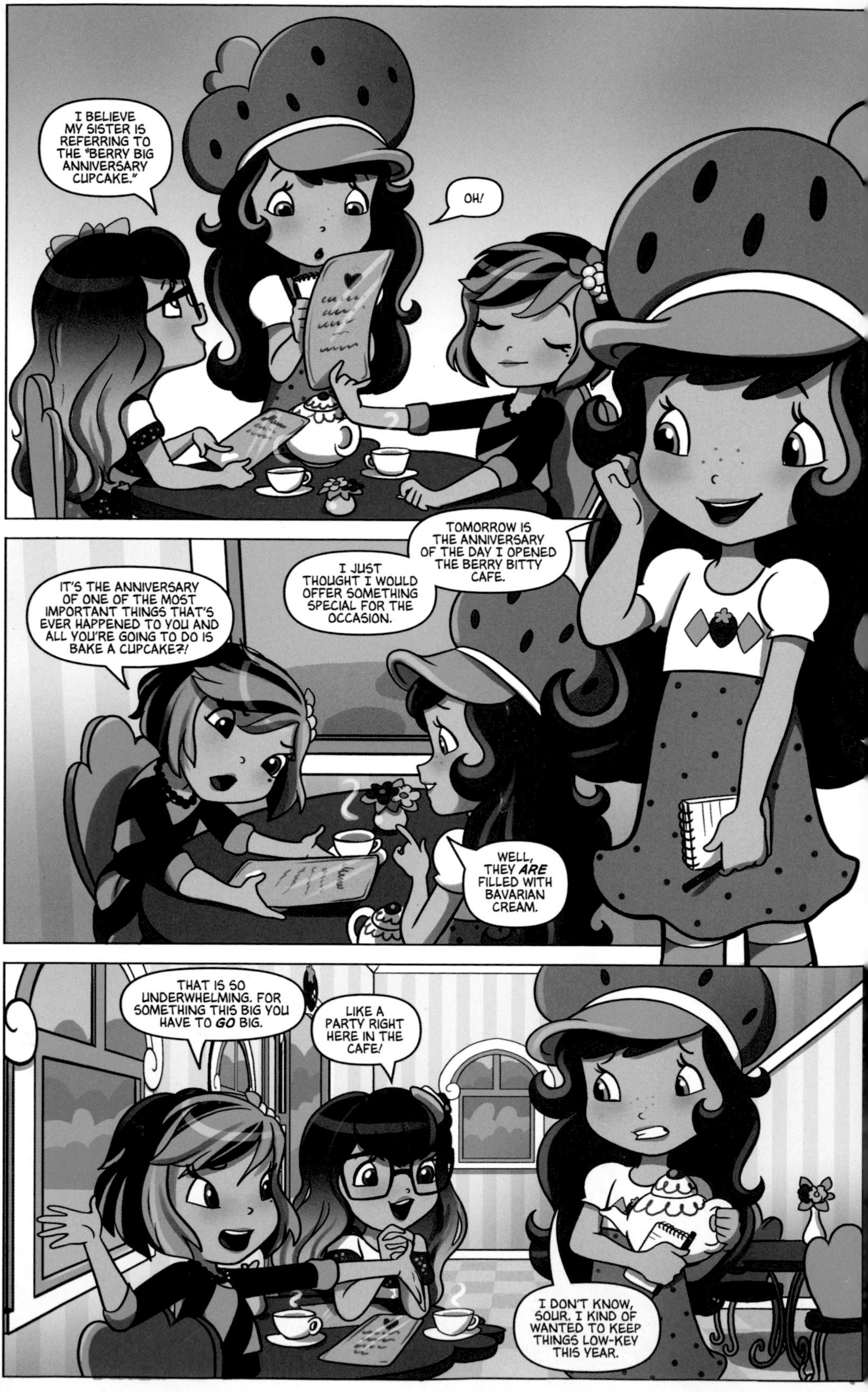
I BELIEVE MY SISTER IS REFERRING TO THE "BERRY BIG ANNIVERSARY CUPCAKE."
OH!
TOMORROW IS THE ANNIVERSARY OF THE DAY I OPENED THE BERRY BITTY CAFE.
I JUST THOUGHT I WOULD OFFER SOMETHING SPECIAL FOR THE OCCASION.
IT'S THE ANNIVERSARY OF ONE OF THE MOST IMPORTANT THINGS THAT'S EVER HAPPENED TO YOU AND ALL YOU'RE GOING TO DO IS BAKE A CUPCAKE?!
WELL, THEY *ARE* FILLED WITH BAVARIAN CREAM.
THAT IS SO UNDERWHELMING. FOR SOMETHING THIS BIG YOU HAVE TO *GO* BIG.
LIKE A PARTY RIGHT HERE IN THE CAFE!
I DON'T KNOW, SOUR. I KIND OF WANTED TO KEEP THINGS LOW-KEY THIS YEAR.

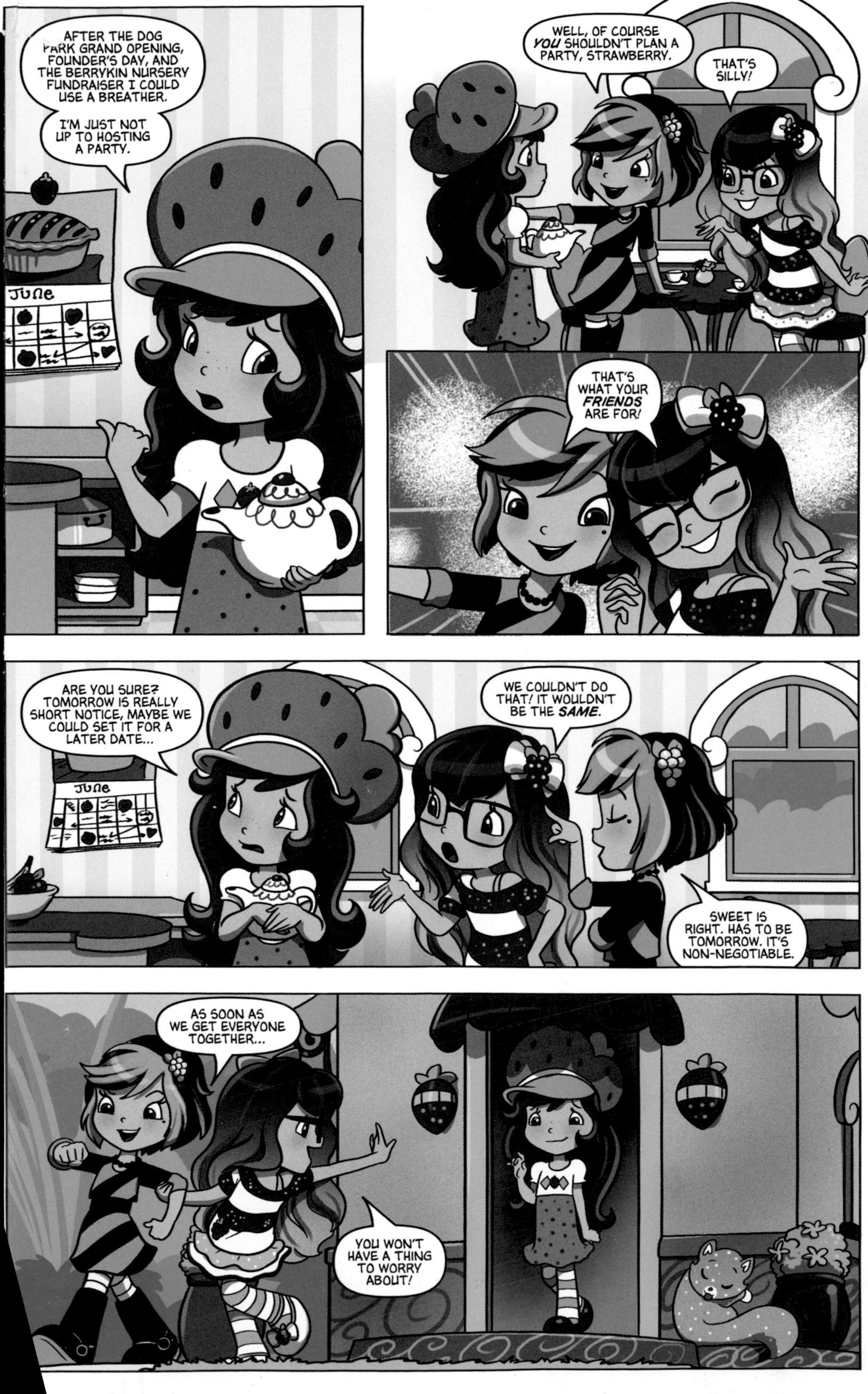

AFTER THE DOG PARK GRAND OPENING, FOUNDER'S DAY, AND THE BERRYKIN NURSERY FUNDRAISER I COULD USE A BREATHER.
I'M JUST NOT UP TO HOSTING A PARTY.
WELL, OF COURSE YOU SHOULDN'T PLAN A PARTY, STRAWBERRY.
THAT'S SILLY!
THAT'S WHAT YOUR FRIENDS ARE FOR!
ARE YOU SURE? TOMORROW IS REALLY SHORT NOTICE, MAYBE WE COULD SET IT FOR A LATER DATE...
WE COULDN'T DO THAT! IT WOULDN'T BE THE SAME.
SWEET IS RIGHT. HAS TO BE TOMORROW. IT'S NON-NEGOTIABLE.
AS SOON AS WE GET EVERYONE TOGETHER...
YOU WON'T HAVE A THING TO WORRY ABOUT!

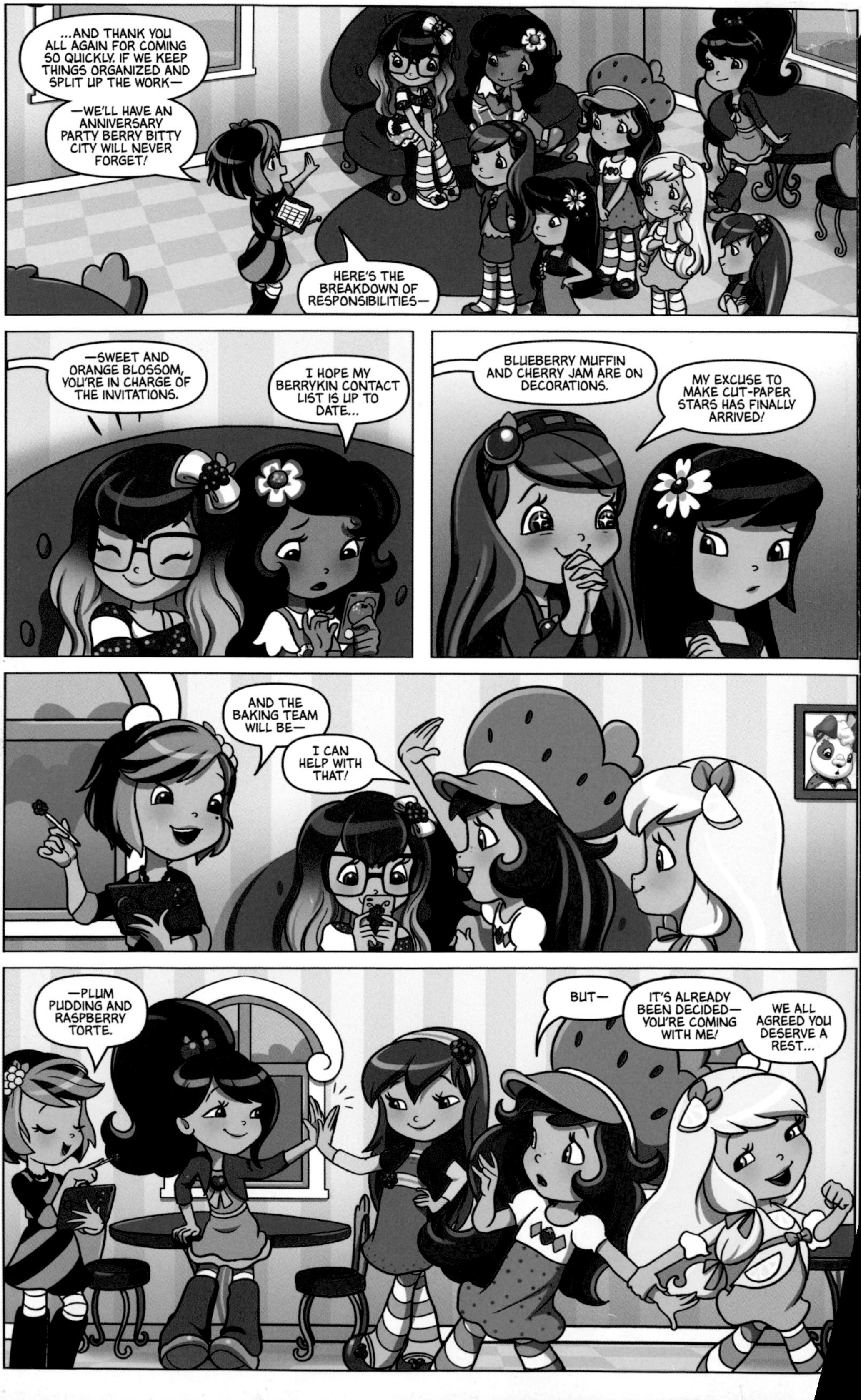
...AND THANK YOU ALL AGAIN FOR COMING SO QUICKLY. IF WE KEEP THINGS ORGANIZED AND SPLIT UP THE WORK—
—WE'LL HAVE AN ANNIVERSARY PARTY BERRY BITTY CITY WILL NEVER FORGET!
HERE'S THE BREAKDOWN OF RESPONSIBILITIES—
—SWEET AND ORANGE BLOSSOM, YOU'RE IN CHARGE OF THE INVITATIONS.
I HOPE MY BERRYKIN CONTACT LIST IS UP TO DATE...
BLUEBERRY MUFFIN AND CHERRY JAM ARE ON DECORATIONS.
MY EXCUSE TO MAKE CUT-PAPER STARS HAS FINALLY ARRIVED!
AND THE BAKING TEAM WILL BE—
I CAN HELP WITH THAT!
—PLUM PUDDING AND RASPBERRY TORTE.
BUT—
IT'S ALREADY BEEN DECIDED— YOU'RE COMING WITH ME!
WE ALL AGREED YOU DESERVE A REST...

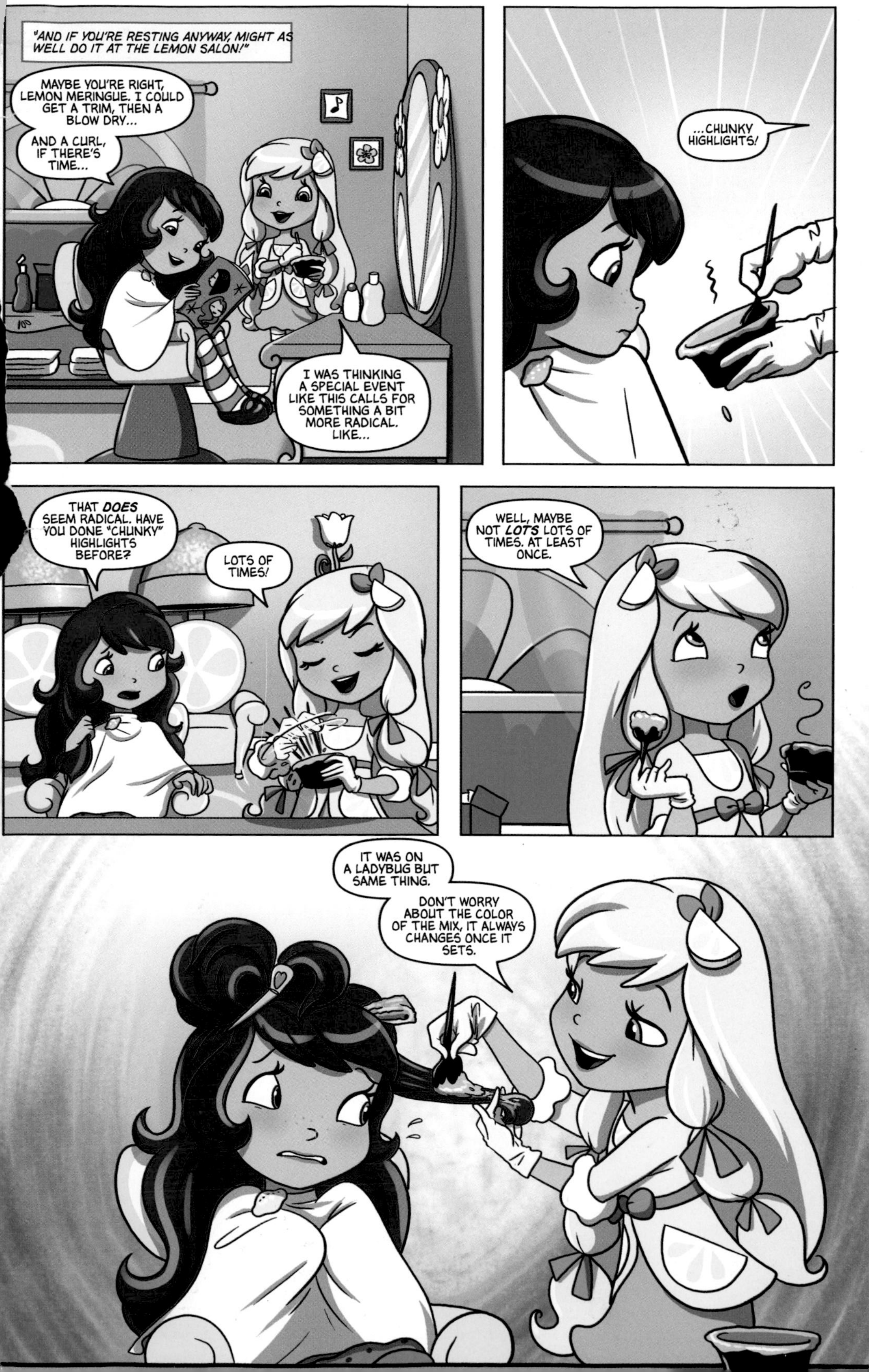
"AND IF YOU'RE RESTING ANYWAY, MIGHT AS WELL DO IT AT THE LEMON SALON!"
MAYBE YOU'RE RIGHT, LEMON MERINGUE. I COULD GET A TRIM, THEN A BLOW DRY...
AND A CURL, IF THERE'S TIME...
I WAS THINKING A SPECIAL EVENT LIKE THIS CALLS FOR SOMETHING A BIT MORE RADICAL. LIKE...
...CHUNKY HIGHLIGHTS!
THAT *DOES* SEEM RADICAL. HAVE YOU DONE "CHUNKY" HIGHLIGHTS BEFORE?
LOTS OF TIMES!
WELL, MAYBE NOT *LOTS* LOTS OF TIMES. AT LEAST ONCE.
IT WAS ON A LADYBUG BUT SAME THING.
DON'T WORRY ABOUT THE COLOR OF THE MIX, IT ALWAYS CHANGES ONCE IT SETS.

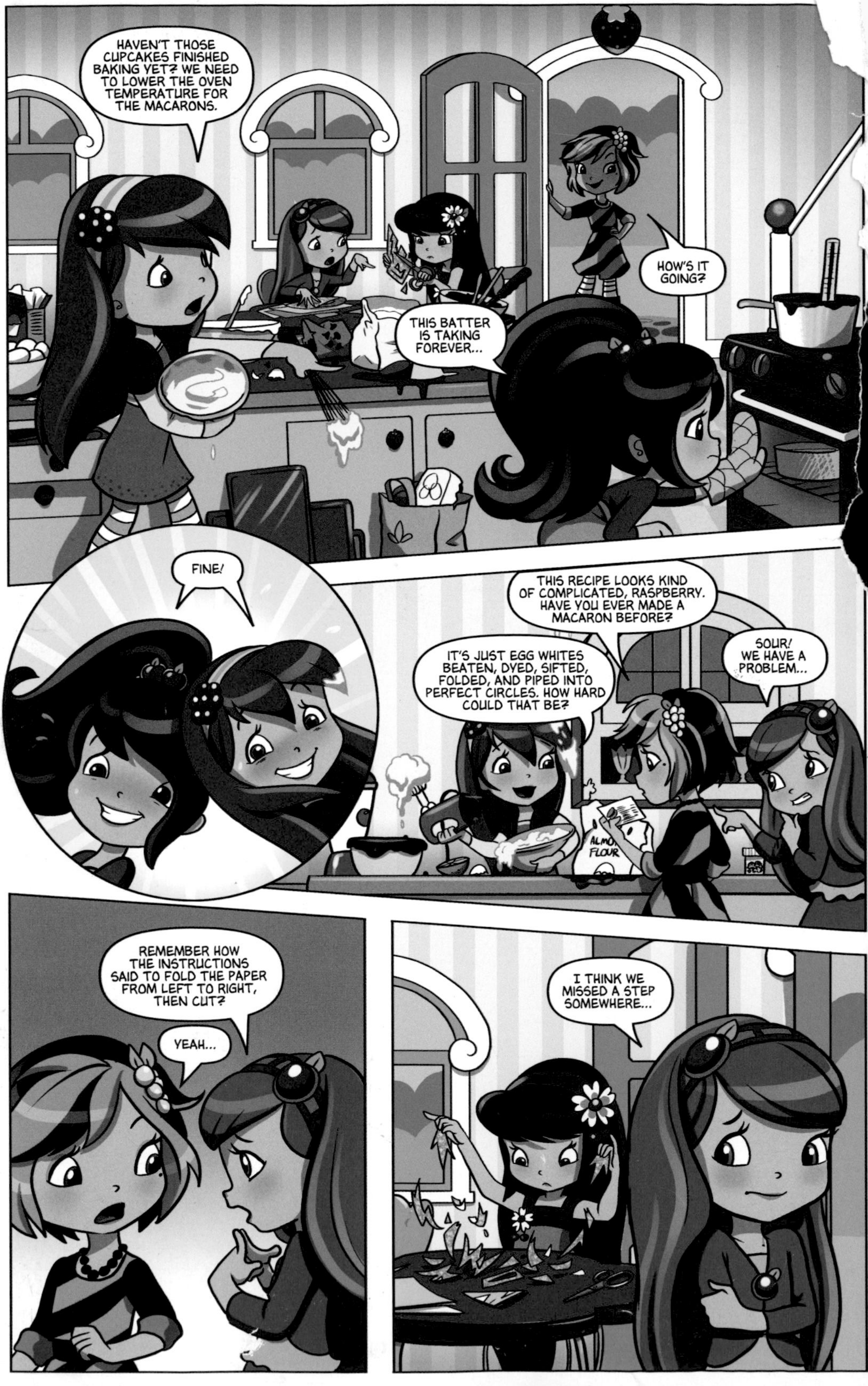
HAVEN'T THOSE CUPCAKES FINISHED BAKING YET? WE NEED TO LOWER THE OVEN TEMPERATURE FOR THE MACARONS.
HOW'S IT GOING?
THIS BATTER IS TAKING FOREVER...
FINE!
THIS RECIPE LOOKS KIND OF COMPLICATED, RASPBERRY. HAVE YOU EVER MADE A MACARON BEFORE?
IT'S JUST EGG WHITES BEATEN, DYED, SIFTED, FOLDED, AND PIPED INTO PERFECT CIRCLES. HOW HARD COULD THAT BE?
SOUR! WE HAVE A PROBLEM...
REMEMBER HOW THE INSTRUCTIONS SAID TO FOLD THE PAPER FROM LEFT TO RIGHT, THEN CUT?
YEAH...
I THINK WE MISSED A STEP SOMEWHERE...

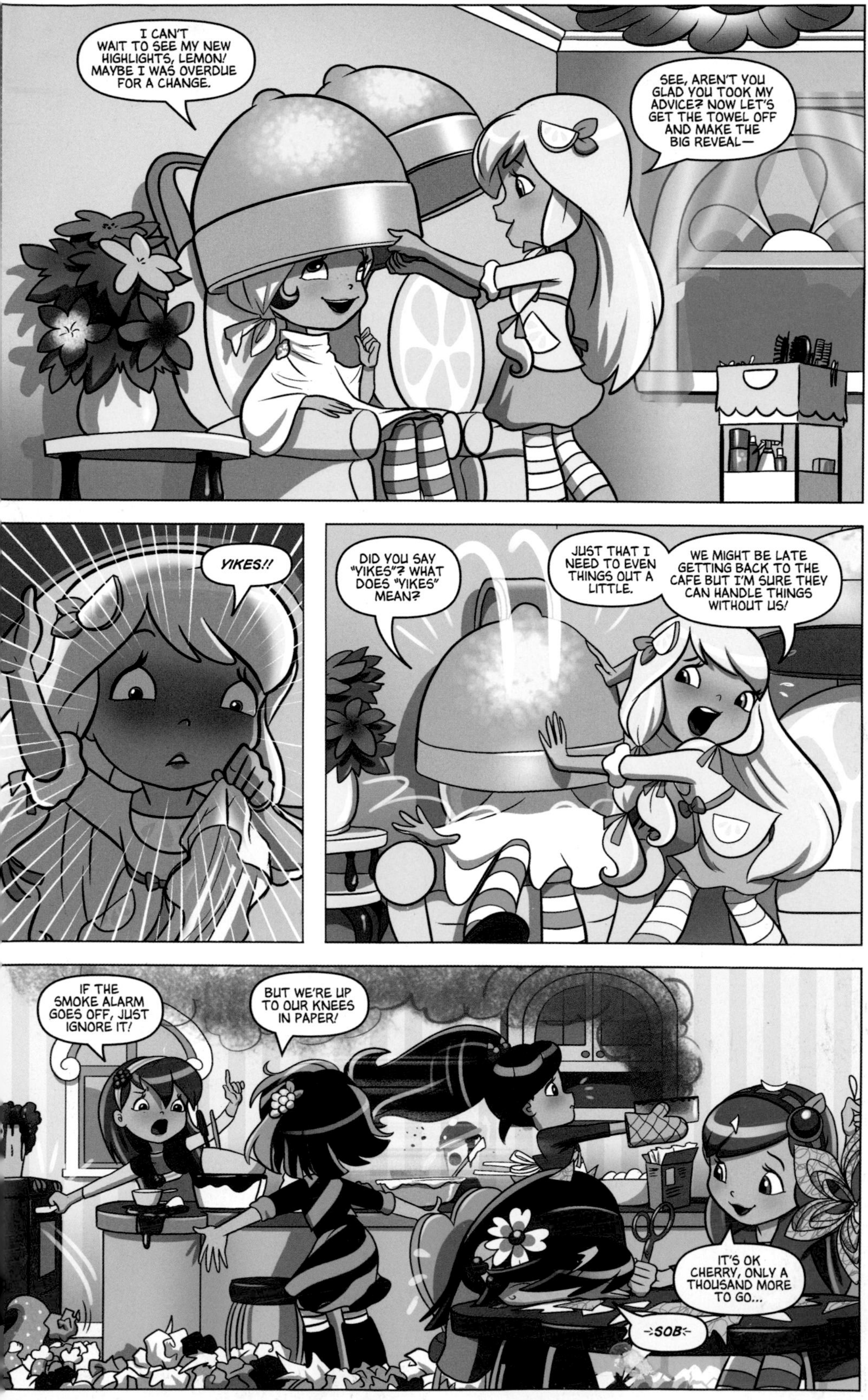
I CAN'T WAIT TO SEE MY NEW HIGHLIGHTS, LEMON! MAYBE I WAS OVERDUE FOR A CHANGE.
SEE, AREN'T YOU GLAD YOU TOOK MY ADVICE? NOW LET'S GET THE TOWEL OFF AND MAKE THE BIG REVEAL—
YIKES!!
DID YOU SAY "YIKES"? WHAT DOES "YIKES" MEAN?
JUST THAT I NEED TO EVEN THINGS OUT A LITTLE.
WE MIGHT BE LATE GETTING BACK TO THE CAFE BUT I'M SURE THEY CAN HANDLE THINGS WITHOUT US!
IF THE SMOKE ALARM GOES OFF, JUST IGNORE IT!
BUT WE'RE UP TO OUR KNEES IN PAPER!
IT'S OK CHERRY, ONLY A THOUSAND MORE TO GO...
SOB

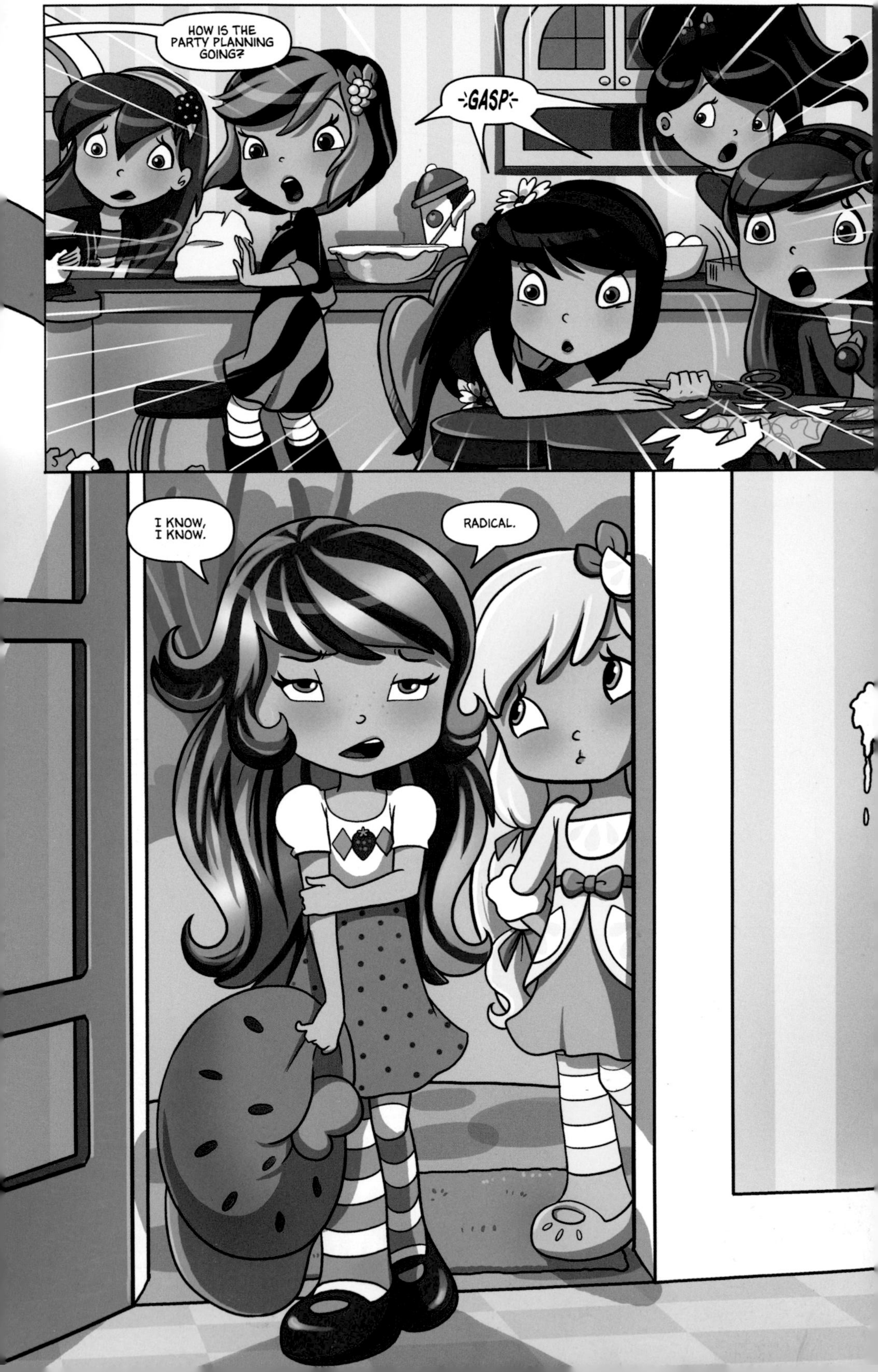
HOW IS THE PARTY PLANNING GOING?
-GASP-
I KNOW, I KNOW.
RADICAL.

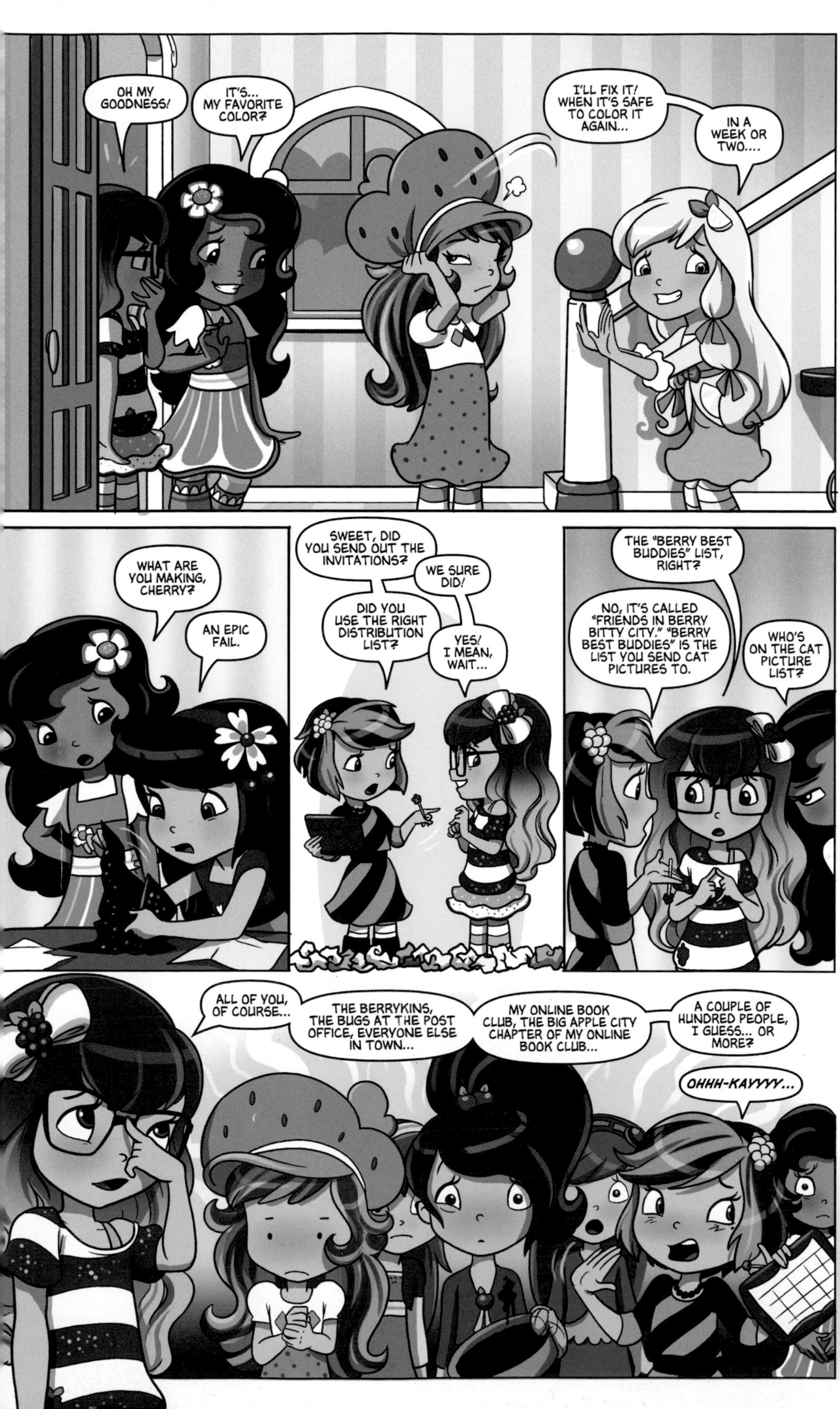
OH MY GOODNESS!
IT'S... MY FAVORITE COLOR?
I'LL FIX IT! WHEN IT'S SAFE TO COLOR IT AGAIN...
IN A WEEK OR TWO....
WHAT ARE YOU MAKING, CHERRY?
AN EPIC FAIL.
SWEET, DID YOU SEND OUT THE INVITATIONS?
WE SURE DID!
DID YOU USE THE RIGHT DISTRIBUTION LIST?
YES! I MEAN, WAIT...
THE "BERRY BEST BUDDIES" LIST, RIGHT?
NO, IT'S CALLED "FRIENDS IN BERRY BITTY CITY." "BERRY BEST BUDDIES" IS THE LIST YOU SEND CAT PICTURES TO.
WHO'S ON THE CAT PICTURE LIST?
ALL OF YOU, OF COURSE...
THE BERRYKINS, THE BUGS AT THE POST OFFICE, EVERYONE ELSE IN TOWN...
MY ONLINE BOOK CLUB, THE BIG APPLE CITY CHAPTER OF MY ONLINE BOOK CLUB...
A COUPLE OF HUNDRED PEOPLE, I GUESS... OR MORE?
OHHH-KAYYYY...

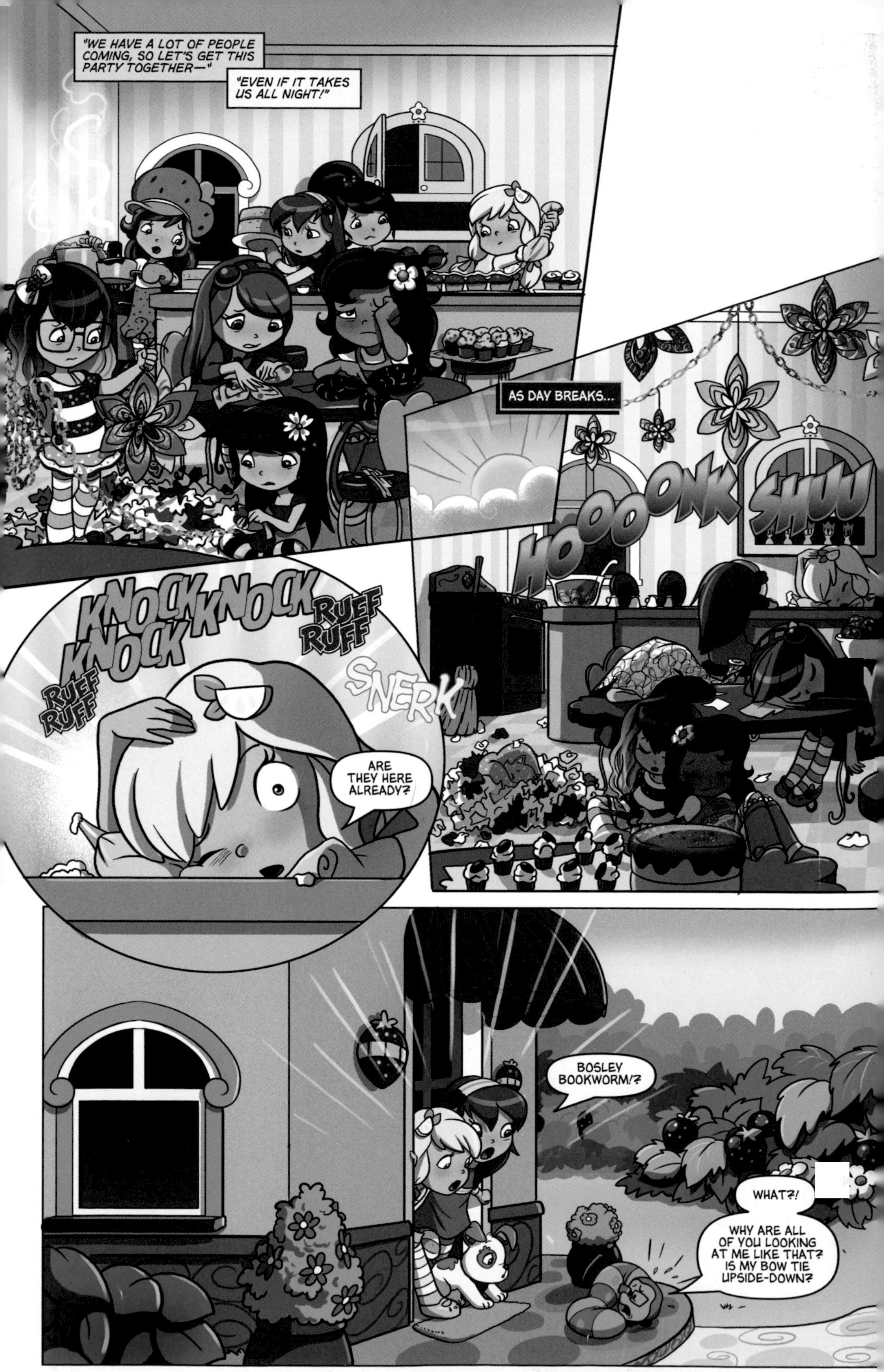
"WE HAVE A LOT OF PEOPLE COMING, SO LET'S GET THIS PARTY TOGETHER—"
"EVEN IF IT TAKES US ALL NIGHT!"
AS DAY BREAKS...
HOOOOONK
SHUU
KNOCK KNOCK
KNOCK KNOCK
RUFF RUFF
RUFF RUFF
SNERK
ARE THEY HERE ALREADY?
BOSLEY BOOKWORM!?
WHAT?!
WHY ARE ALL OF YOU LOOKING AT ME LIKE THAT? IS MY BOW TIE UPSIDE-DOWN?

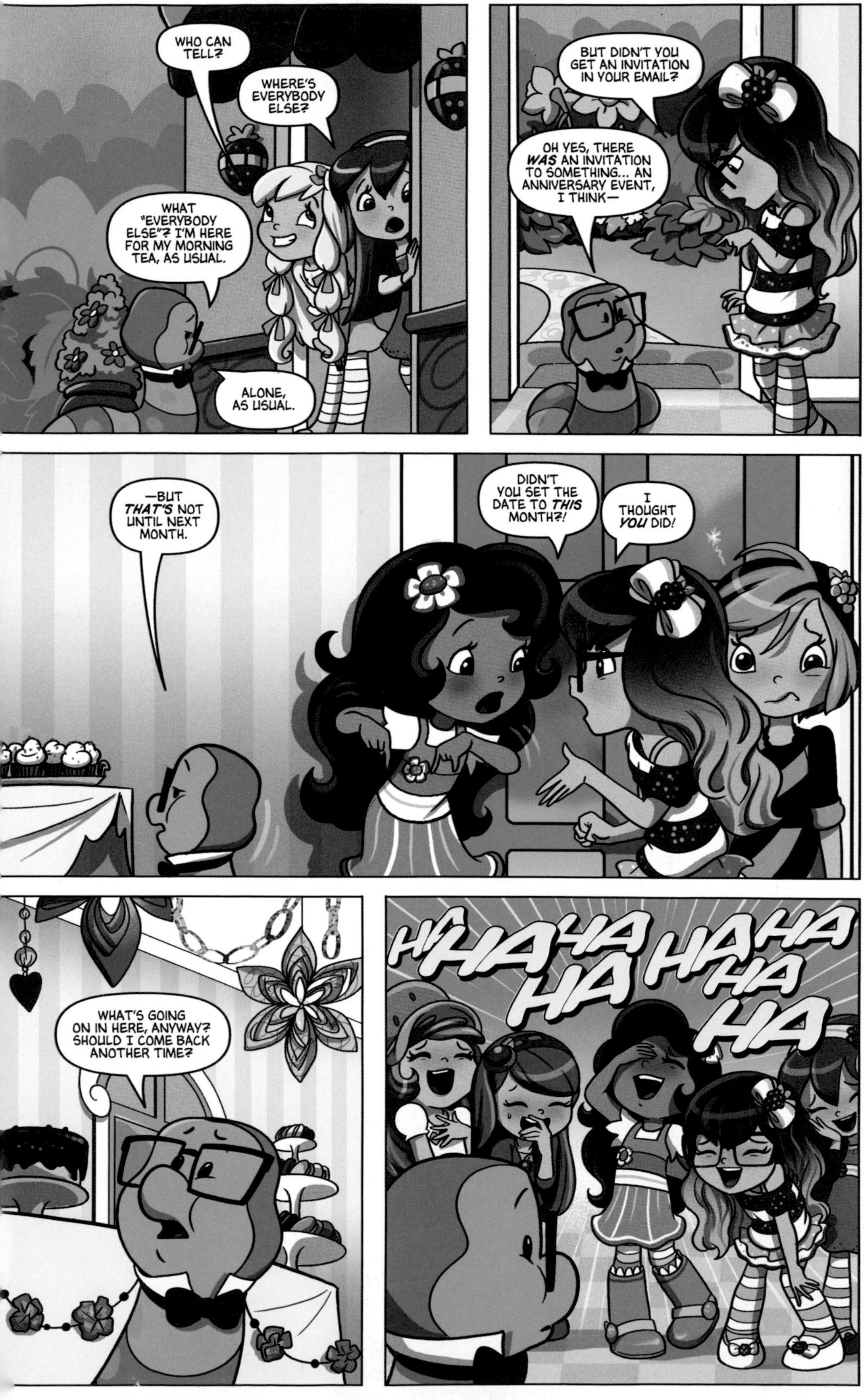
WHO CAN TELL?
WHERE'S EVERYBODY ELSE?
WHAT "EVERYBODY ELSE"? I'M HERE FOR MY MORNING TEA, AS USUAL.
ALONE, AS USUAL.
BUT DIDN'T YOU GET AN INVITATION IN YOUR EMAIL?
OH YES, THERE WAS AN INVITATION TO SOMETHING... AN ANNIVERSARY EVENT, I THINK—
—BUT THAT'S NOT UNTIL NEXT MONTH.
DIDN'T YOU SET THE DATE TO THIS MONTH?!
I THOUGHT YOU DID!
WHAT'S GOING ON IN HERE, ANYWAY? SHOULD I COME BACK ANOTHER TIME?
HAHAHA HAHAHA HA HA HA HA

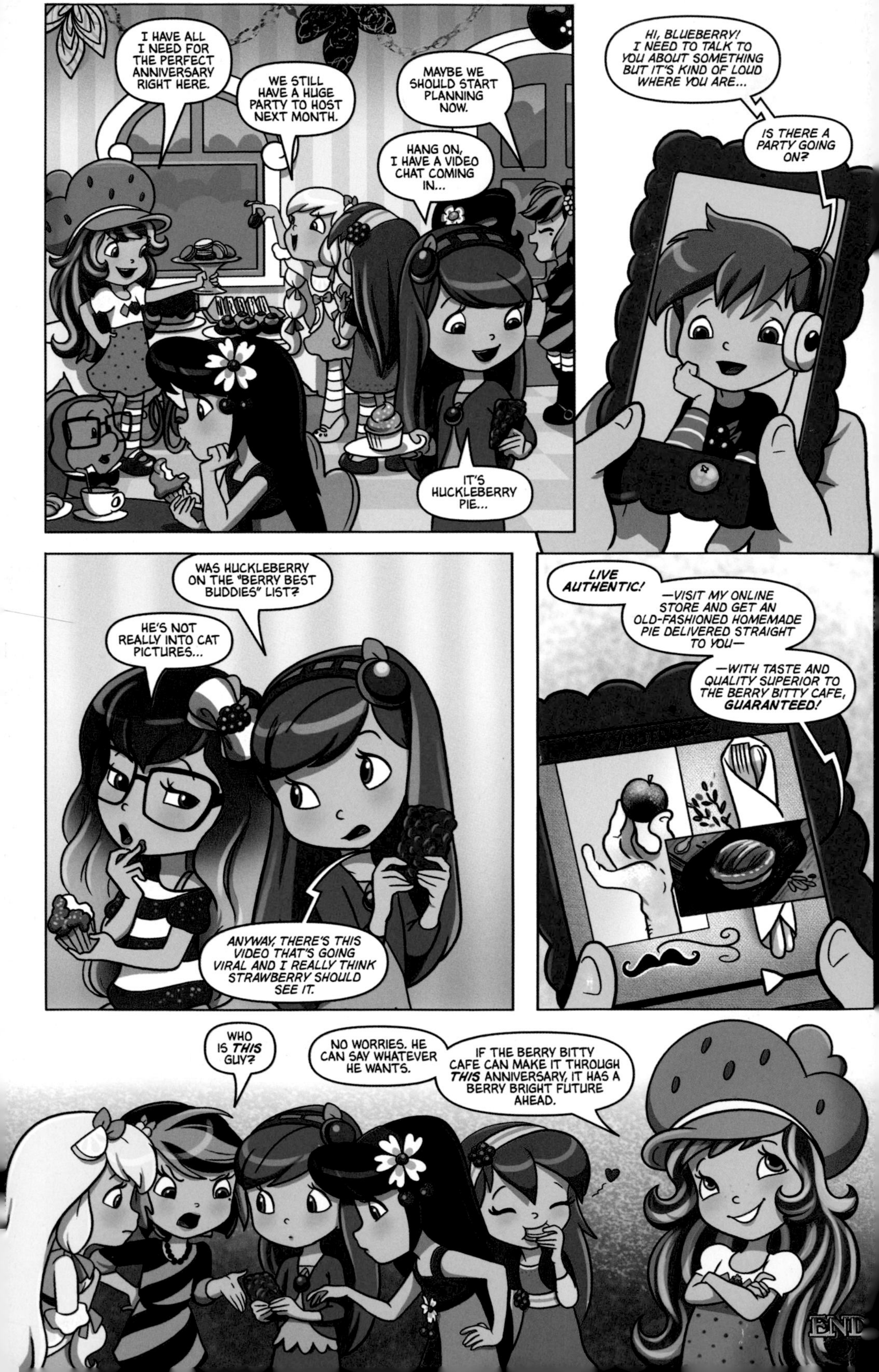
I HAVE ALL I NEED FOR THE PERFECT ANNIVERSARY RIGHT HERE.
WE STILL HAVE A HUGE PARTY TO HOST NEXT MONTH.
MAYBE WE SHOULD START PLANNING NOW.
HANG ON, I HAVE A VIDEO CHAT COMING IN...
IT'S HUCKLEBERRY PIE...
HI, BLUEBERRY! I NEED TO TALK TO YOU ABOUT SOMETHING BUT IT'S KIND OF LOUD WHERE YOU ARE...
IS THERE A PARTY GOING ON?
WAS HUCKLEBERRY ON THE "BERRY BEST BUDDIES" LIST?
HE'S NOT REALLY INTO CAT PICTURES...
ANYWAY, THERE'S THIS VIDEO THAT'S GOING VIRAL AND I REALLY THINK STRAWBERRY SHOULD SEE IT.
LIVE AUTHENTIC!
—VISIT MY ONLINE STORE AND GET AN OLD-FASHIONED HOMEMADE PIE DELIVERED STRAIGHT TO YOU—
—WITH TASTE AND QUALITY SUPERIOR TO THE BERRY BITTY CAFE, GUARANTEED!
WHO IS THIS GUY?
NO WORRIES. HE CAN SAY WHATEVER HE WANTS.
IF THE BERRY BITTY CAFE CAN MAKE IT THROUGH THIS ANNIVERSARY, IT HAS A BERRY BRIGHT FUTURE AHEAD.
END

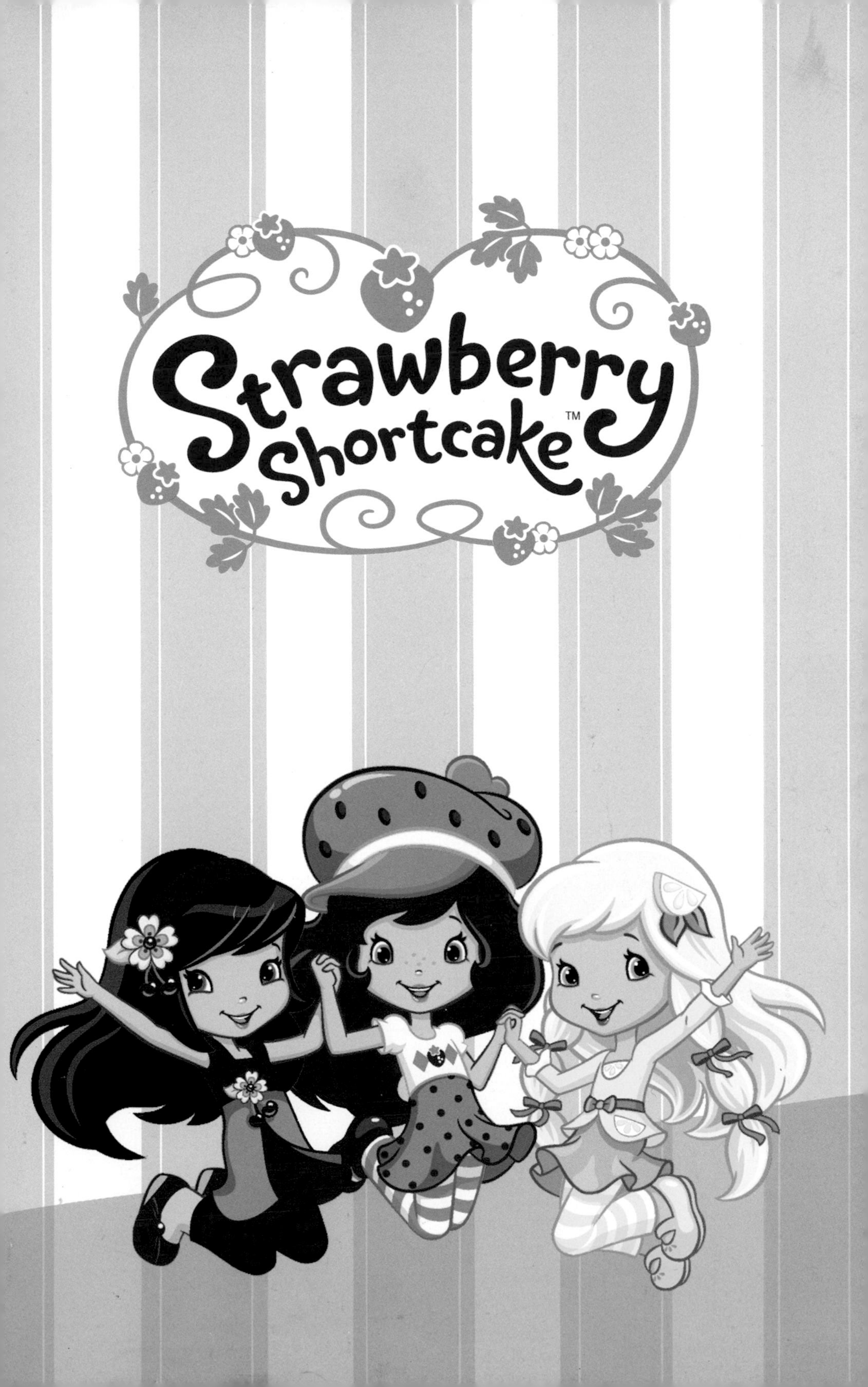
Strawberry Shortcake™

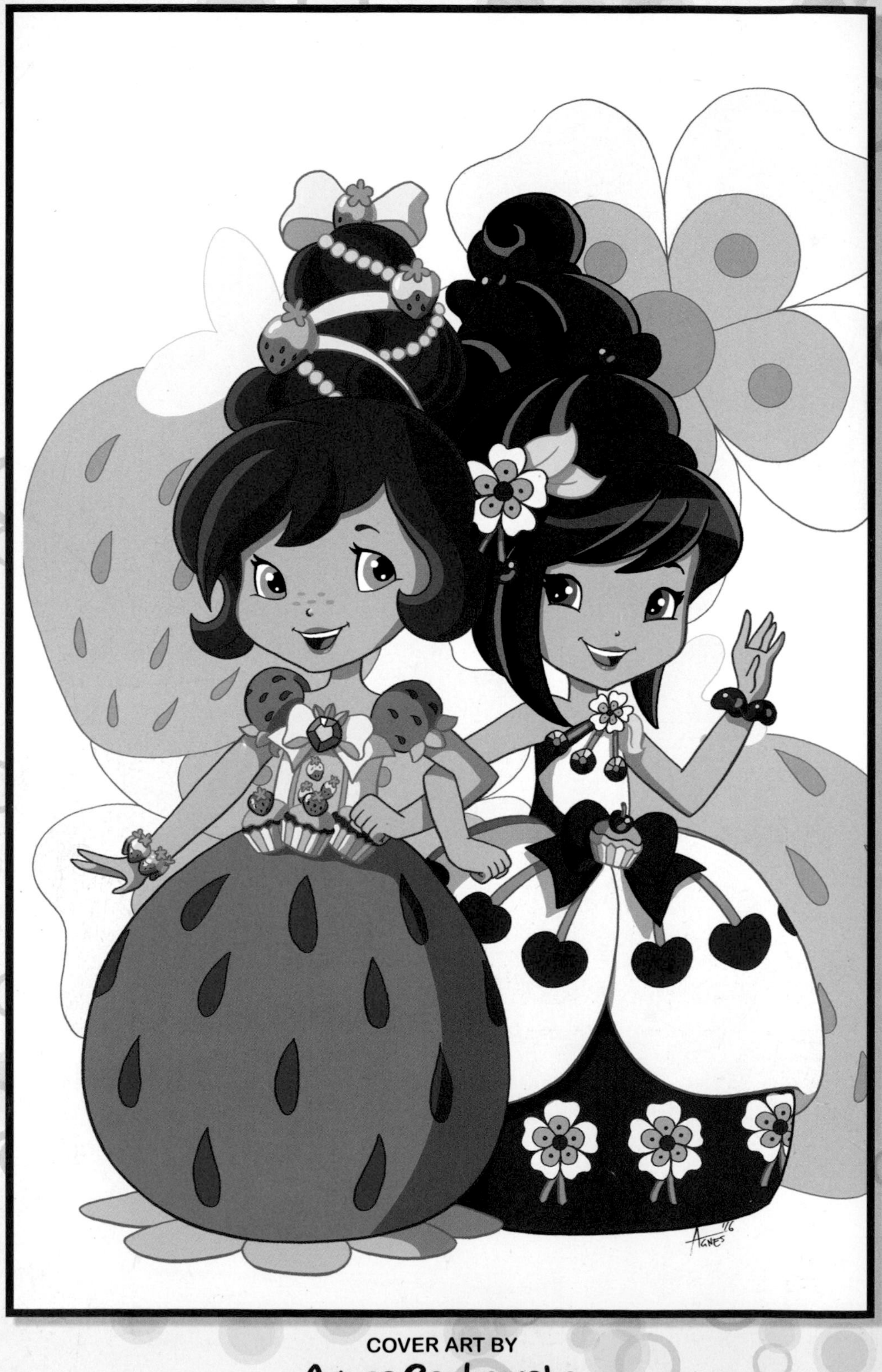
AGNES '16

COVER ART BY
Agnes Garbowska

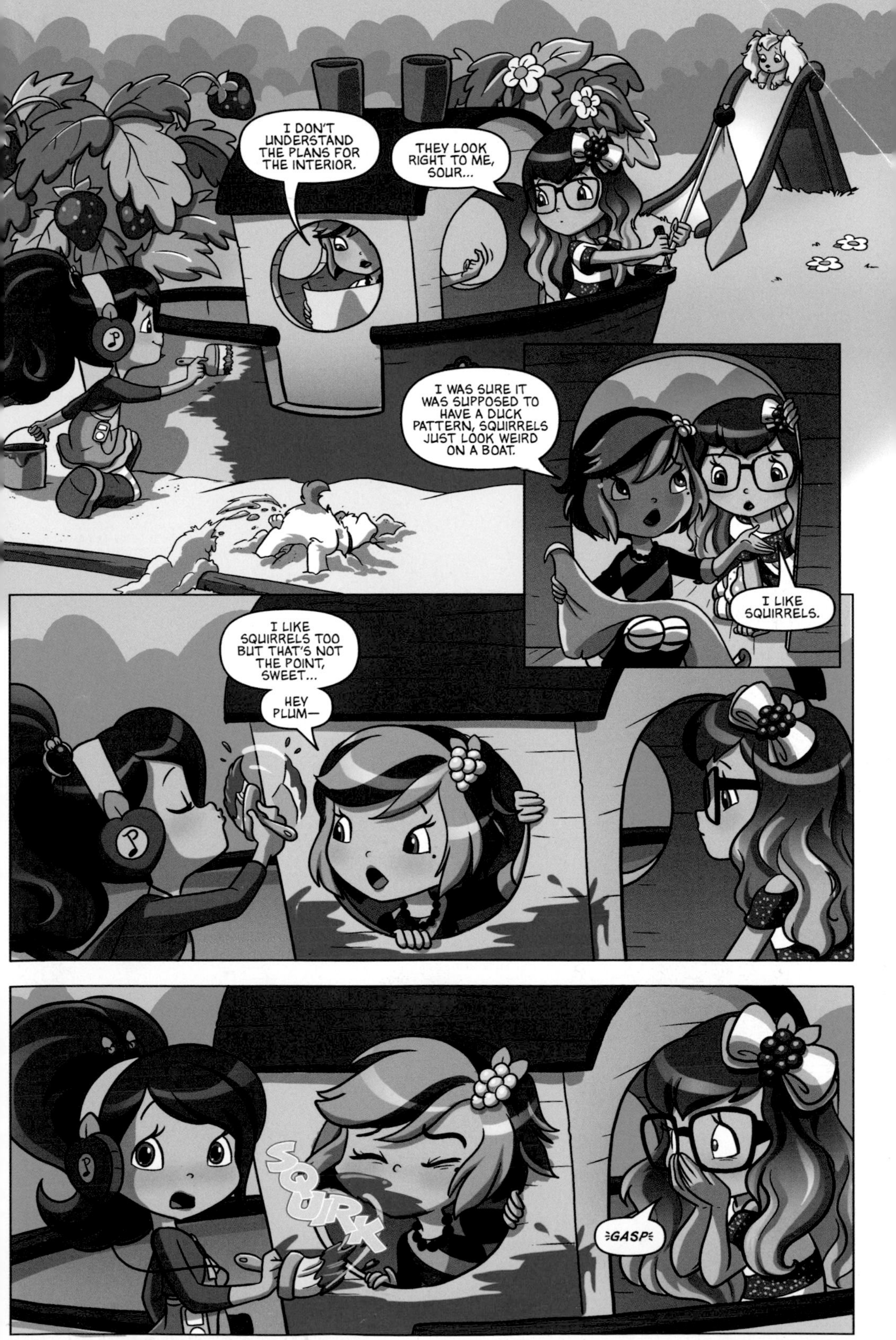
I DON'T UNDERSTAND THE PLANS FOR THE INTERIOR.
THEY LOOK RIGHT TO ME, SOUR...
I WAS SURE IT WAS SUPPOSED TO HAVE A DUCK PATTERN, SQUIRRELS JUST LOOK WEIRD ON A BOAT.
I LIKE SQUIRRELS.
I LIKE SQUIRRELS TOO BUT THAT'S NOT THE POINT, SWEET...
HEY PLUM—
SQUIRK
GASP

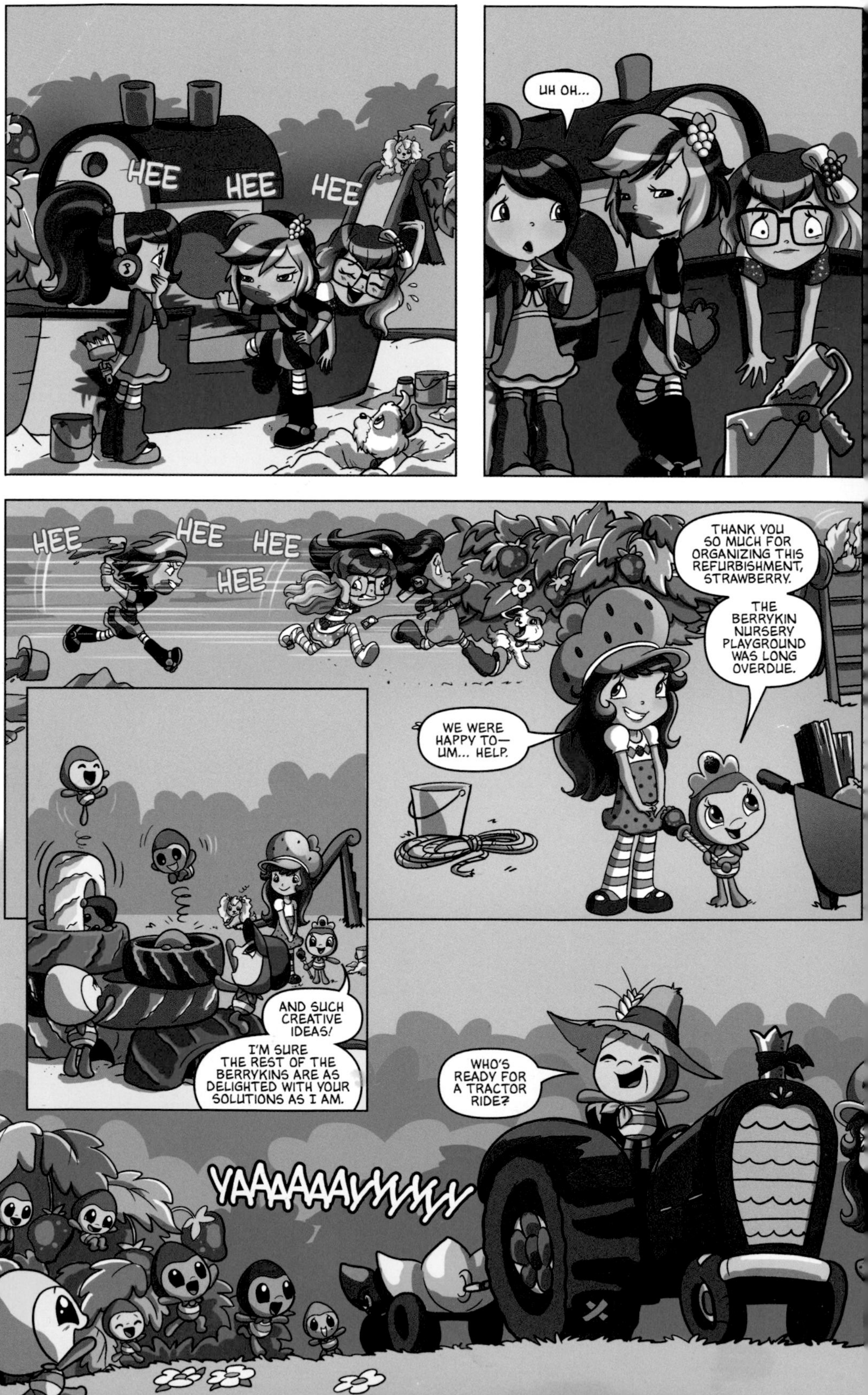
HEE
HEE
HEE
UH OH...
HEE
HEE
HEE
HEE
THANK YOU SO MUCH FOR ORGANIZING THIS REFURBISHMENT, STRAWBERRY.
THE BERRYKIN NURSERY PLAYGROUND WAS LONG OVERDUE.
WE WERE HAPPY TO— UM... HELP.
AND SUCH CREATIVE IDEAS!
I'M SURE THE REST OF THE BERRYKINS ARE AS DELIGHTED WITH YOUR SOLUTIONS AS I AM.
WHO'S READY FOR A TRACTOR RIDE?
YAAAAAAYYYYY

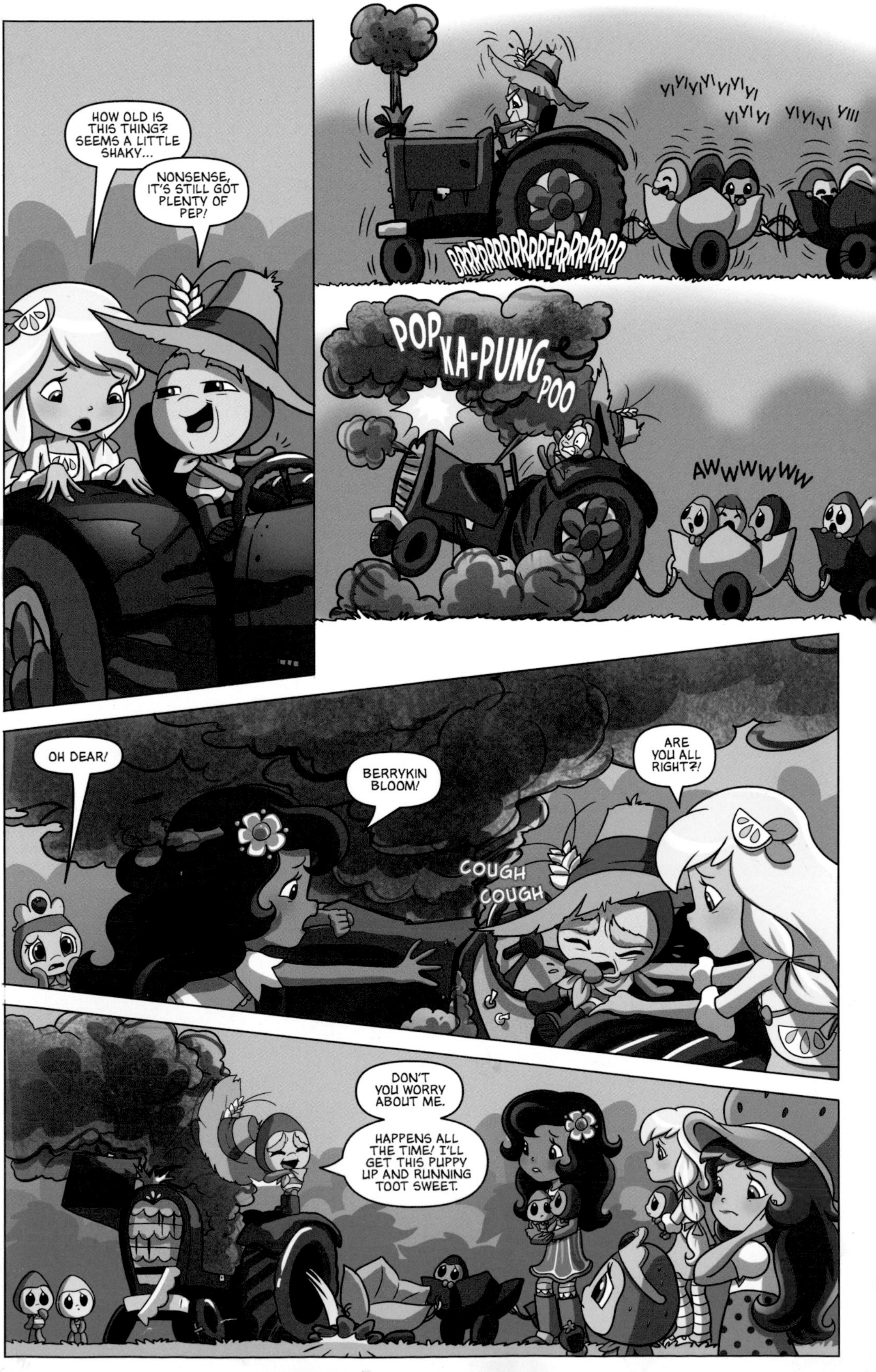
HOW OLD IS THIS THING? SEEMS A LITTLE SHAKY...
NONSENSE, IT'S STILL GOT PLENTY OF PEP!
YIYIYIYIYIYIYI
YIYIYI
YIYIYI YIII
BRRRRRRRRRRRERRRRRRR
POP
KA-PUNG
POO
AWWWWWW
OH DEAR!
BERRYKIN BLOOM!
ARE YOU ALL RIGHT?!
COUGH
COUGH
DON'T YOU WORRY ABOUT ME.
HAPPENS ALL THE TIME! I'LL GET THIS PUPPY UP AND RUNNING TOOT SWEET.

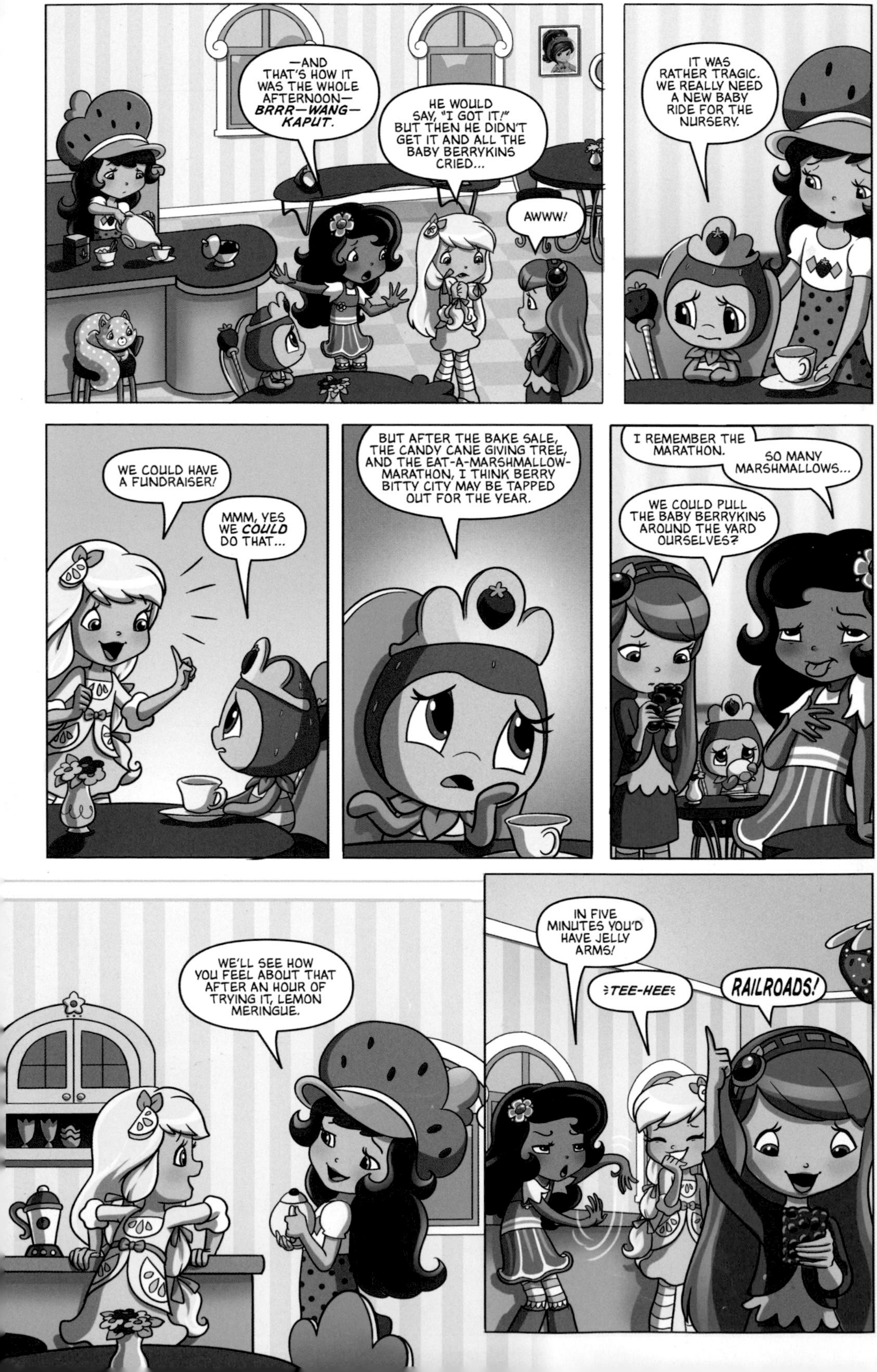
—AND THAT'S HOW IT WAS THE WHOLE AFTERNOON— BRRR—WANG— KAPUT.
HE WOULD SAY, "I GOT IT!" BUT THEN HE DIDN'T GET IT AND ALL THE BABY BERRYKINS CRIED...
AWWW!
IT WAS RATHER TRAGIC. WE REALLY NEED A NEW BABY RIDE FOR THE NURSERY.
WE COULD HAVE A FUNDRAISER!
MMM, YES WE COULD DO THAT...
BUT AFTER THE BAKE SALE, THE CANDY CANE GIVING TREE, AND THE EAT-A-MARSHMALLOW-MARATHON, I THINK BERRY BITTY CITY MAY BE TAPPED OUT FOR THE YEAR.
I REMEMBER THE MARATHON.
SO MANY MARSHMALLOWS...
WE COULD PULL THE BABY BERRYKINS AROUND THE YARD OURSELVES?
WE'LL SEE HOW YOU FEEL ABOUT THAT AFTER AN HOUR OF TRYING IT, LEMON MERINGUE.
IN FIVE MINUTES YOU'D HAVE JELLY ARMS!
TEE-HEE
RAILROADS!

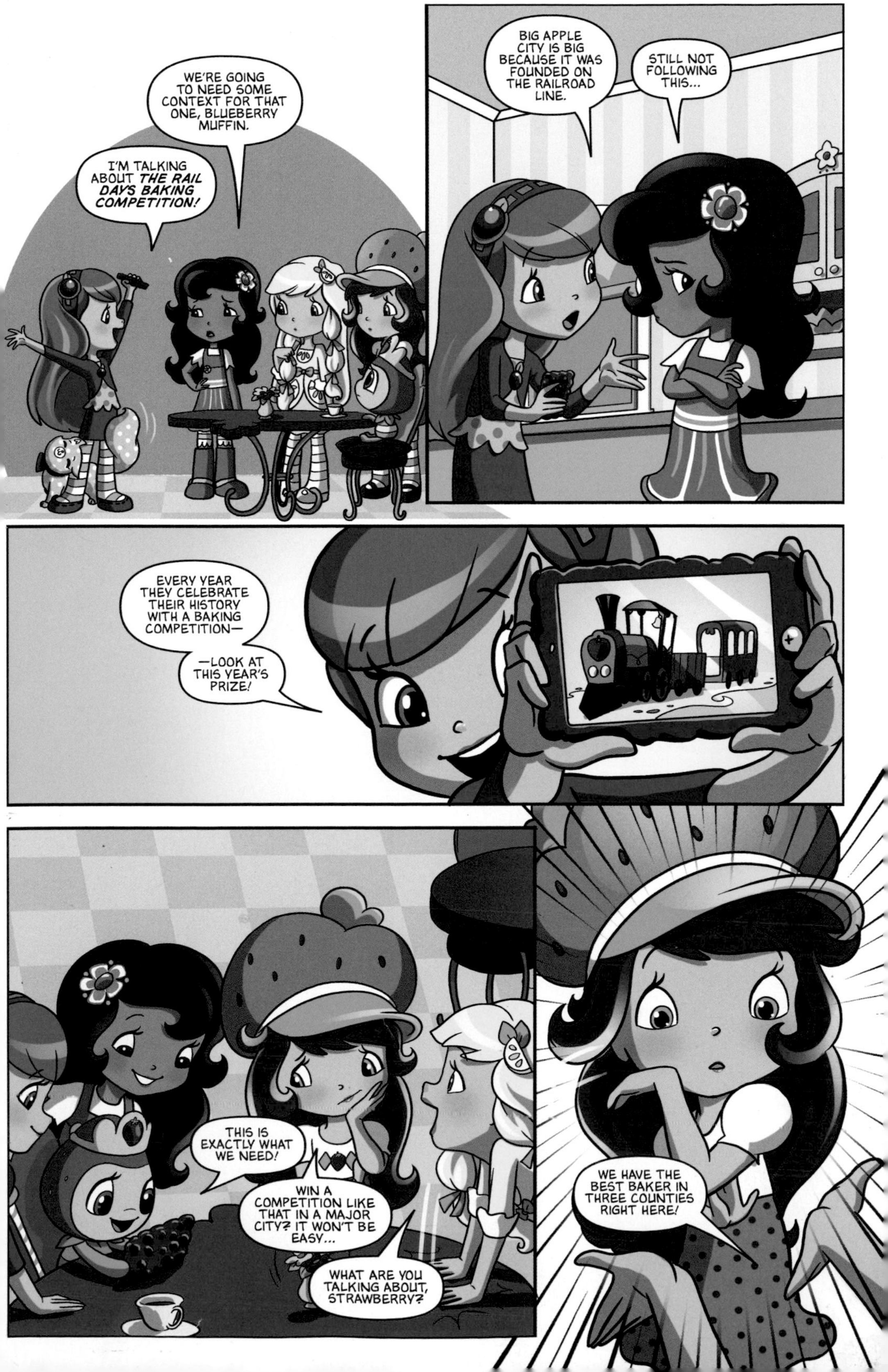

I'M TALKING ABOUT ***THE RAIL DAYS BAKING COMPETITION!***
WE'RE GOING TO NEED SOME CONTEXT FOR THAT ONE, BLUEBERRY MUFFIN.
BIG APPLE CITY IS BIG BECAUSE IT WAS FOUNDED ON THE RAILROAD LINE.
STILL NOT FOLLOWING THIS...
EVERY YEAR THEY CELEBRATE THEIR HISTORY WITH A BAKING COMPETITION—
—LOOK AT THIS YEAR'S PRIZE!
THIS IS EXACTLY WHAT WE NEED!
WIN A COMPETITION LIKE THAT IN A MAJOR CITY? IT WON'T BE EASY...
WHAT ARE YOU TALKING ABOUT, STRAWBERRY?
WE HAVE THE BEST BAKER IN THREE COUNTIES RIGHT HERE!

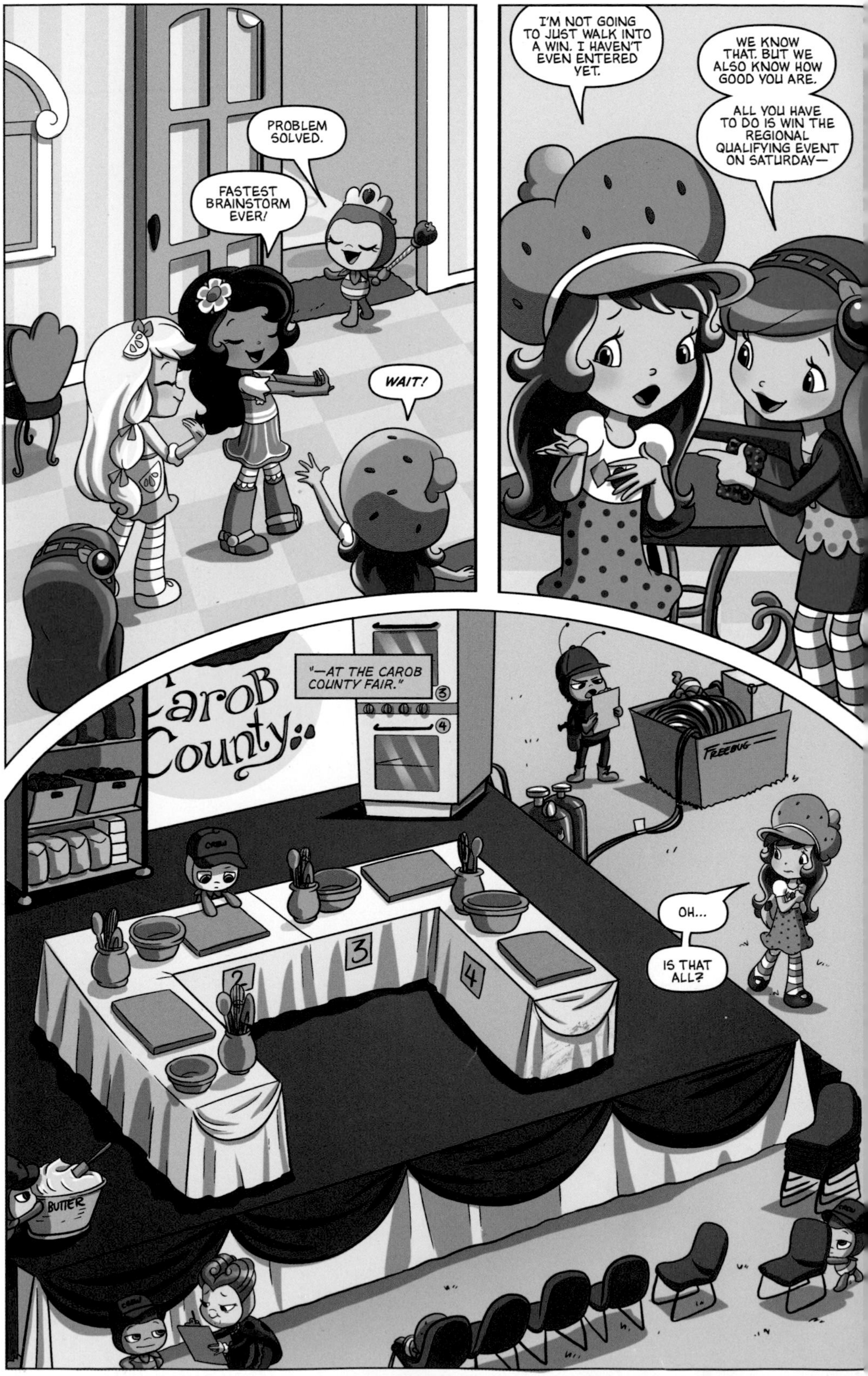
PROBLEM SOLVED.
FASTEST BRAINSTORM EVER!
WAIT!
I'M NOT GOING TO JUST WALK INTO A WIN. I HAVEN'T EVEN ENTERED YET.
WE KNOW THAT. BUT WE ALSO KNOW HOW GOOD YOU ARE.
ALL YOU HAVE TO DO IS WIN THE REGIONAL QUALIFYING EVENT ON SATURDAY—
"—AT THE CAROB COUNTY FAIR."
CaroB County
FREEBUG
BUTTER
OH...
IS THAT ALL?

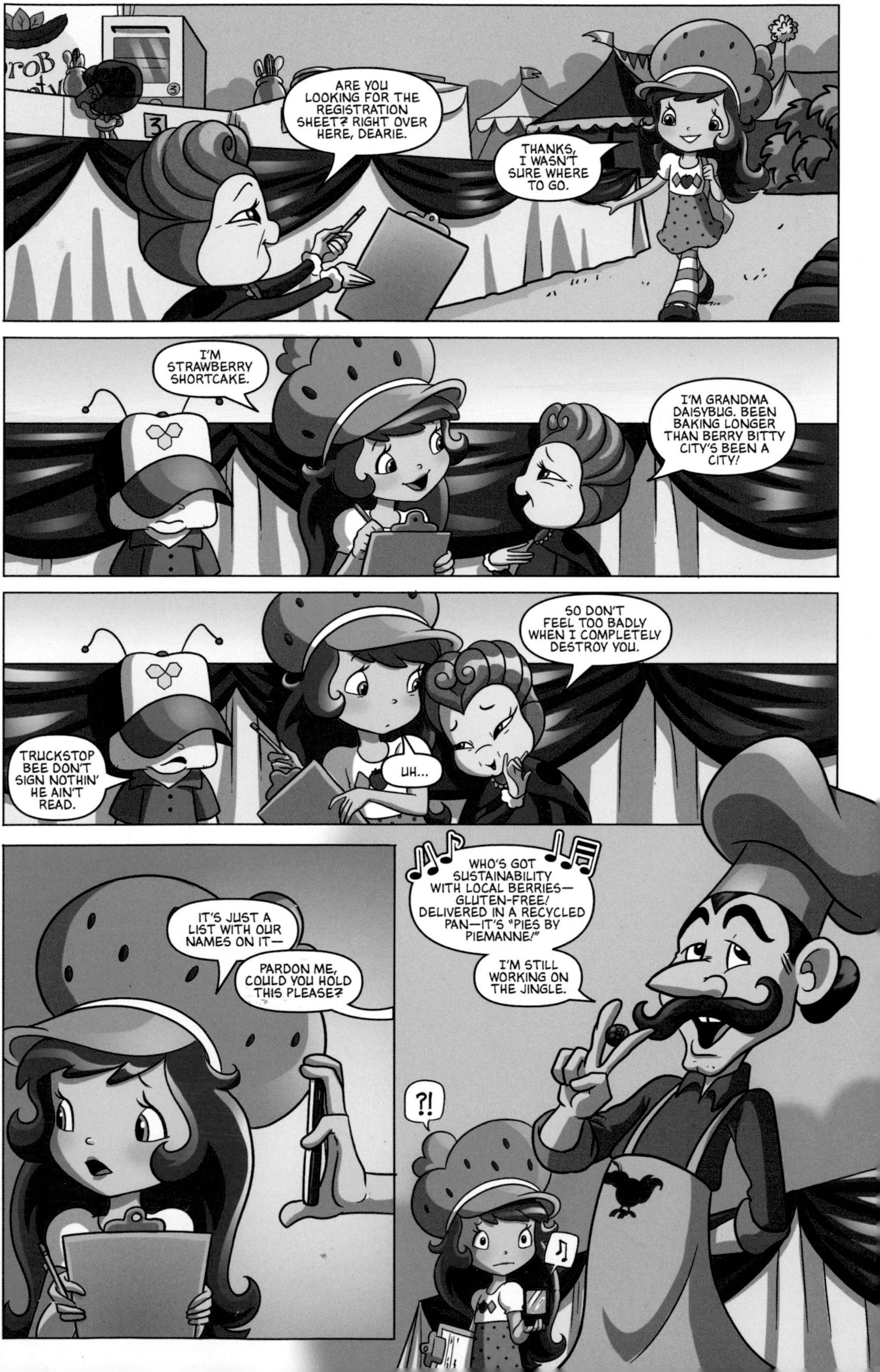
ARE YOU LOOKING FOR THE REGISTRATION SHEET? RIGHT OVER HERE, DEARIE.
THANKS, I WASN'T SURE WHERE TO GO.
I'M STRAWBERRY SHORTCAKE.
I'M GRANDMA DAISYBUG. BEEN BAKING LONGER THAN BERRY BITTY CITY'S BEEN A CITY!
SO DON'T FEEL TOO BADLY WHEN I COMPLETELY DESTROY YOU.
TRUCKSTOP BEE DON'T SIGN NOTHIN' HE AIN'T READ.
UH...
IT'S JUST A LIST WITH OUR NAMES ON IT—
PARDON ME, COULD YOU HOLD THIS PLEASE?
WHO'S GOT SUSTAINABILITY WITH LOCAL BERRIES— GLUTEN-FREE! DELIVERED IN A RECYCLED PAN—IT'S "PIES BY PIEMANNE!"
I'M STILL WORKING ON THE JINGLE.
?!

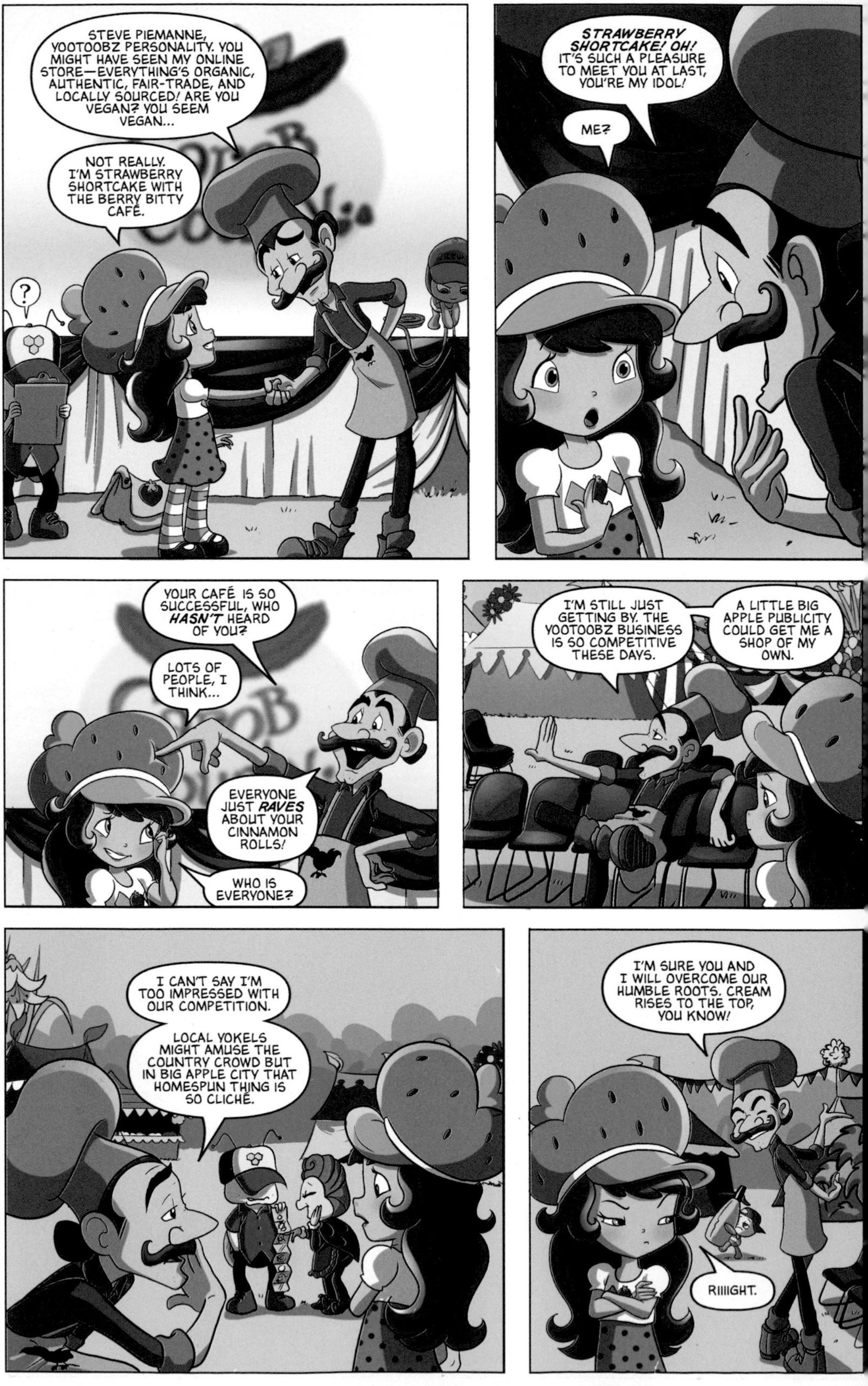
STEVE PIEMANNE, YOOTOOBZ PERSONALITY. YOU MIGHT HAVE SEEN MY ONLINE STORE—EVERYTHING'S ORGANIC, AUTHENTIC, FAIR-TRADE, AND LOCALLY SOURCED! ARE YOU VEGAN? YOU SEEM VEGAN...
NOT REALLY. I'M STRAWBERRY SHORTCAKE WITH THE BERRY BITTY CAFÉ.
?
STRAWBERRY SHORTCAKE! OH! IT'S SUCH A PLEASURE TO MEET YOU AT LAST, YOU'RE MY IDOL!
ME?
YOUR CAFÉ IS SO SUCCESSFUL, WHO HASN'T HEARD OF YOU?
LOTS OF PEOPLE, I THINK...
EVERYONE JUST RAVES ABOUT YOUR CINNAMON ROLLS!
WHO IS EVERYONE?
I'M STILL JUST GETTING BY. THE YOOTOOBZ BUSINESS IS SO COMPETITIVE THESE DAYS.
A LITTLE BIG APPLE PUBLICITY COULD GET ME A SHOP OF MY OWN.
I CAN'T SAY I'M TOO IMPRESSED WITH OUR COMPETITION.
LOCAL YOKELS MIGHT AMUSE THE COUNTRY CROWD BUT IN BIG APPLE CITY THAT HOMESPUN THING IS SO CLICHÉ.
I'M SURE YOU AND I WILL OVERCOME OUR HUMBLE ROOTS. CREAM RISES TO THE TOP, YOU KNOW!
RIIIIGHT.

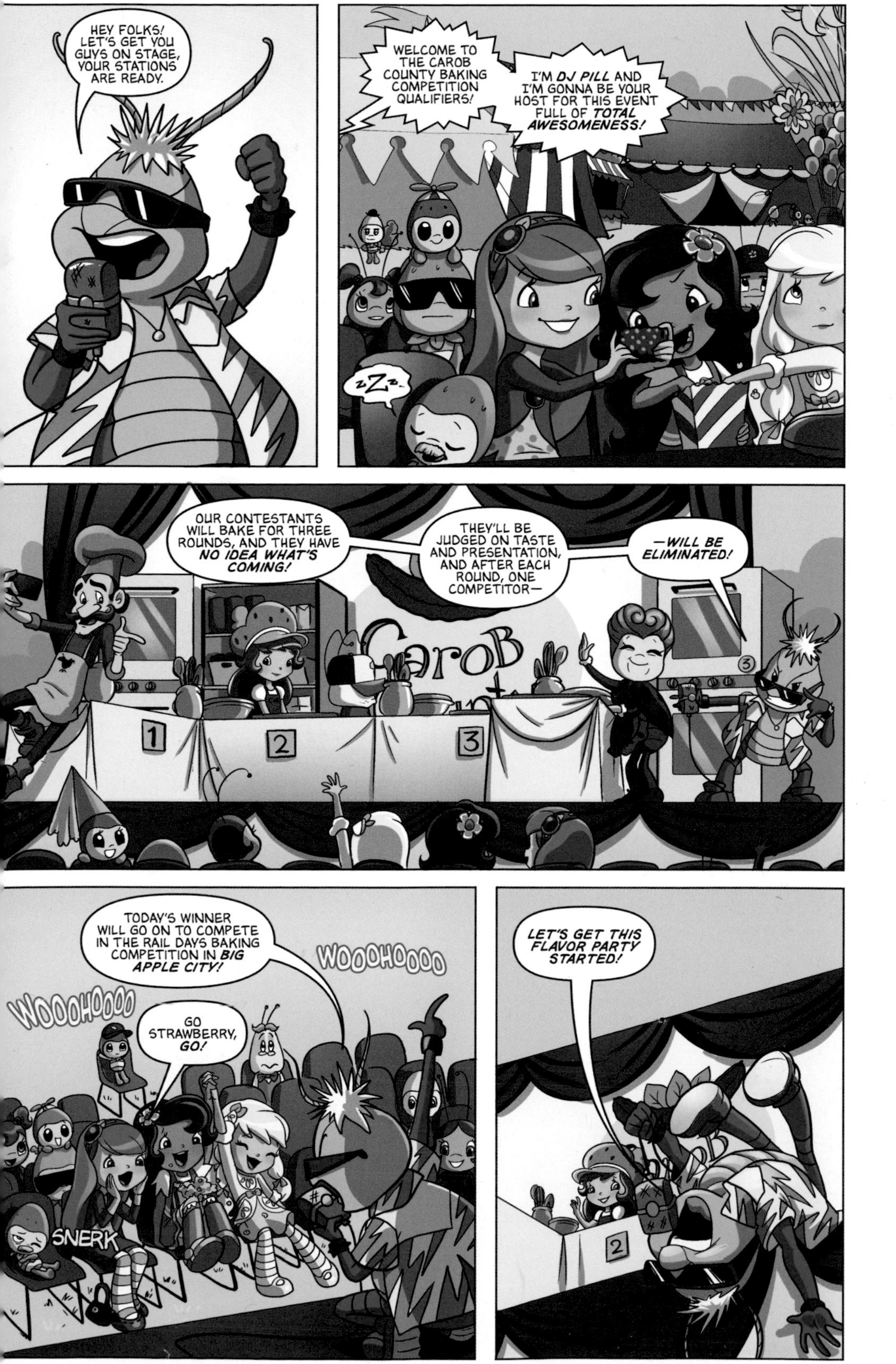
HEY FOLKS! LET'S GET YOU GUYS ON STAGE, YOUR STATIONS ARE READY.
WELCOME TO THE CAROB COUNTY BAKING COMPETITION QUALIFIERS!
I'M *DJ PILL* AND I'M GONNA BE YOUR HOST FOR THIS EVENT FULL OF ***TOTAL AWESOMENESS!***
zZz
OUR CONTESTANTS WILL BAKE FOR THREE ROUNDS, AND THEY HAVE ***NO IDEA WHAT'S COMING!***
THEY'LL BE JUDGED ON TASTE AND PRESENTATION, AND AFTER EACH ROUND, ONE COMPETITOR—
—WILL BE ELIMINATED!
CaroB
1
2
3
TODAY'S WINNER WILL GO ON TO COMPETE IN THE RAIL DAYS BAKING COMPETITION IN ***BIG APPLE CITY!***
WOOOHOOOO
WOOOHOOOO
GO STRAWBERRY, ***GO!***
SNERK
LET'S GET THIS FLAVOR PARTY STARTED!
2

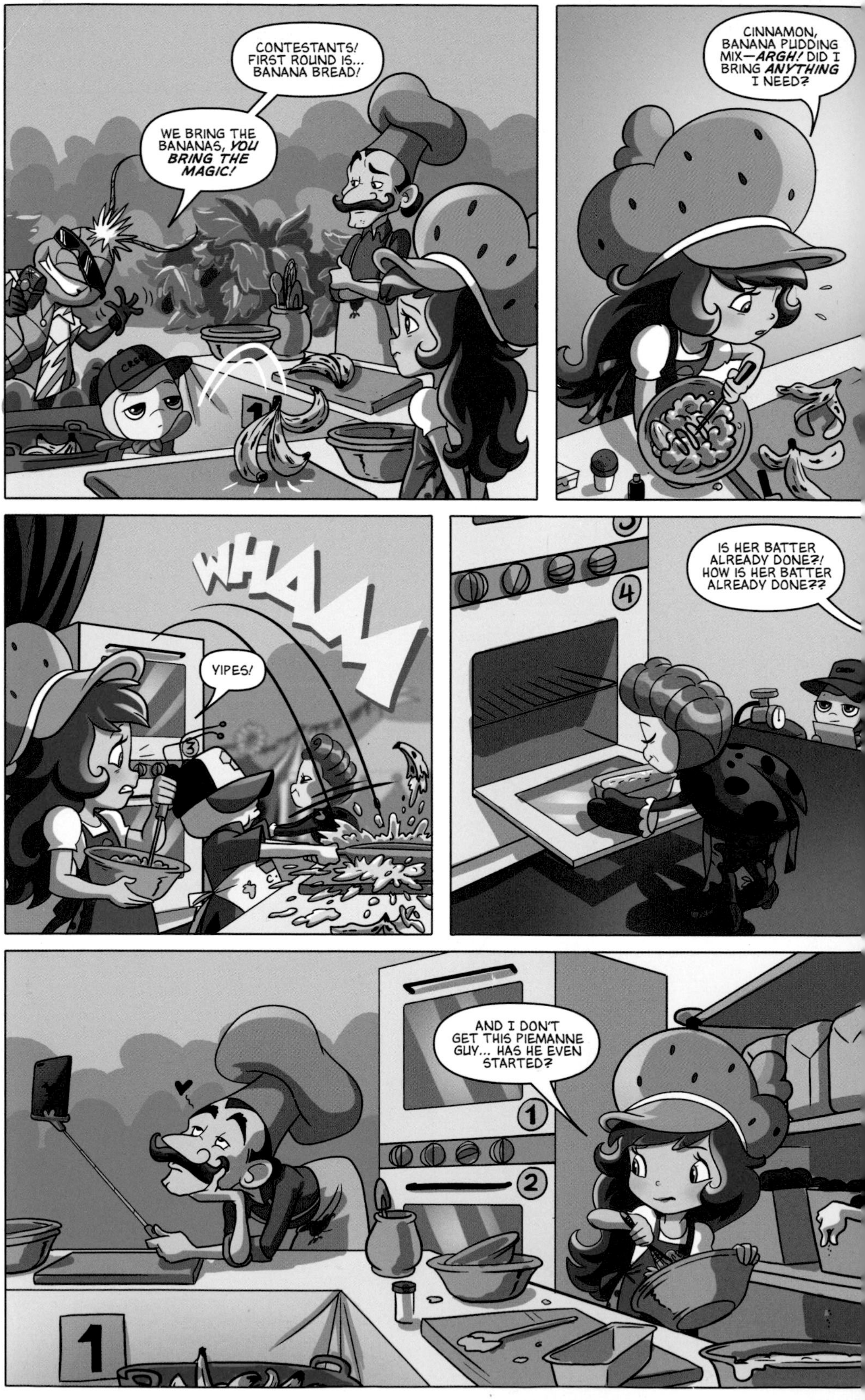
CONTESTANTS! FIRST ROUND IS... BANANA BREAD!
WE BRING THE BANANAS, YOU BRING THE MAGIC!
CREW
1
CINNAMON, BANANA PUDDING MIX—ARGH! DID I BRING ANYTHING I NEED?
WHAM
YIPES!
3
5
4
IS HER BATTER ALREADY DONE?! HOW IS HER BATTER ALREADY DONE??
CREW
AND I DON'T GET THIS PIEMANNE GUY... HAS HE EVEN STARTED?
1
2
1

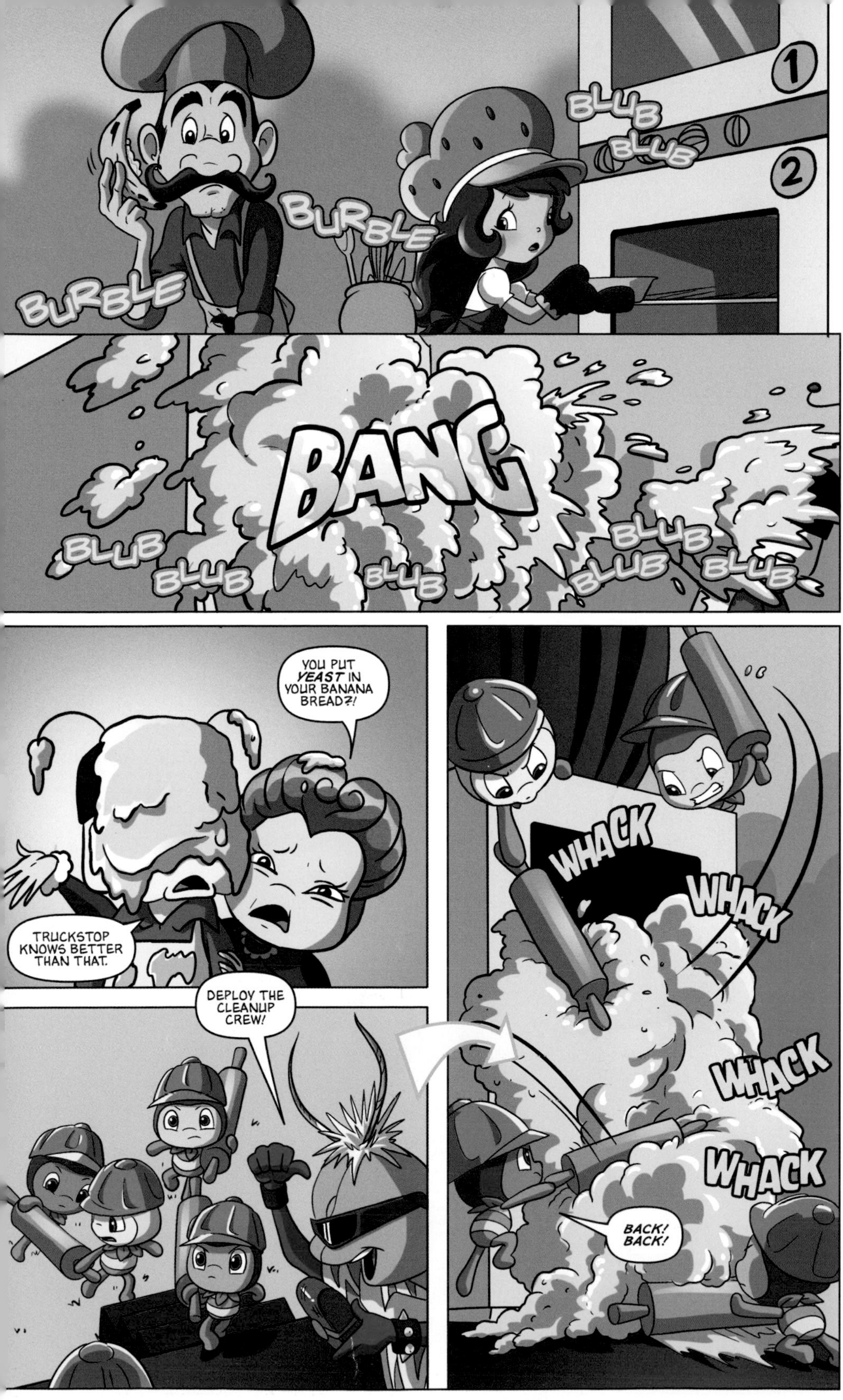
BLUB
BLUB
BURBLE
BURBLE
BANG
BLUB
BLUB
BLUB
BLUB
BLUB
BLUB
YOU PUT *YEAST* IN YOUR BANANA BREAD?!
TRUCKSTOP KNOWS BETTER THAN THAT.
DEPLOY THE CLEANUP CREW!
WHACK
WHACK
WHACK
WHACK
BACK! BACK!

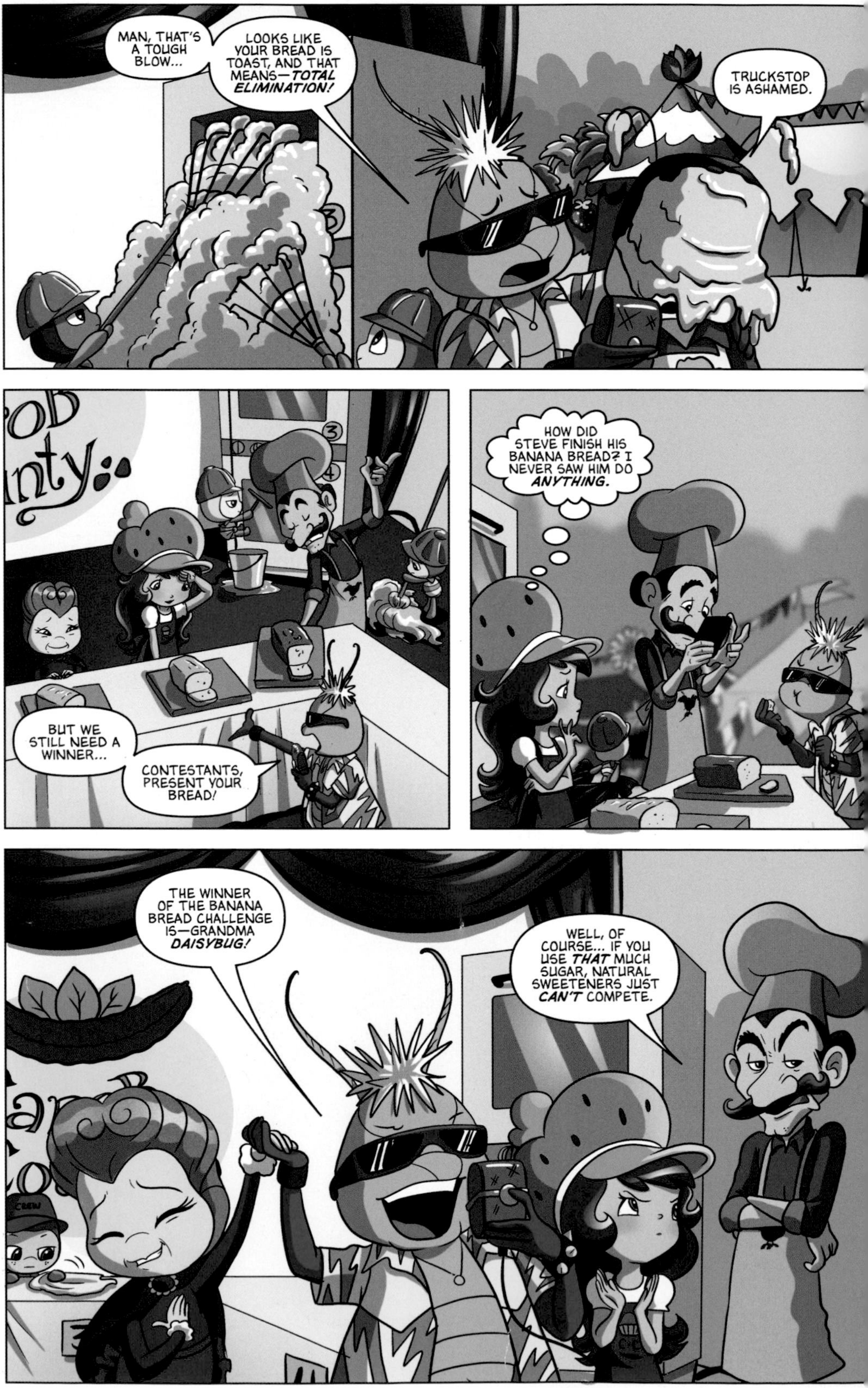
MAN, THAT'S A TOUGH BLOW...
LOOKS LIKE YOUR BREAD IS TOAST, AND THAT MEANS—TOTAL ELIMINATION!
TRUCKSTOP IS ASHAMED.
BUT WE STILL NEED A WINNER...
CONTESTANTS, PRESENT YOUR BREAD!
HOW DID STEVE FINISH HIS BANANA BREAD? I NEVER SAW HIM DO ANYTHING.
THE WINNER OF THE BANANA BREAD CHALLENGE IS—GRANDMA DAISYBUG!
WELL, OF COURSE... IF YOU USE THAT MUCH SUGAR, NATURAL SWEETENERS JUST CAN'T COMPETE.

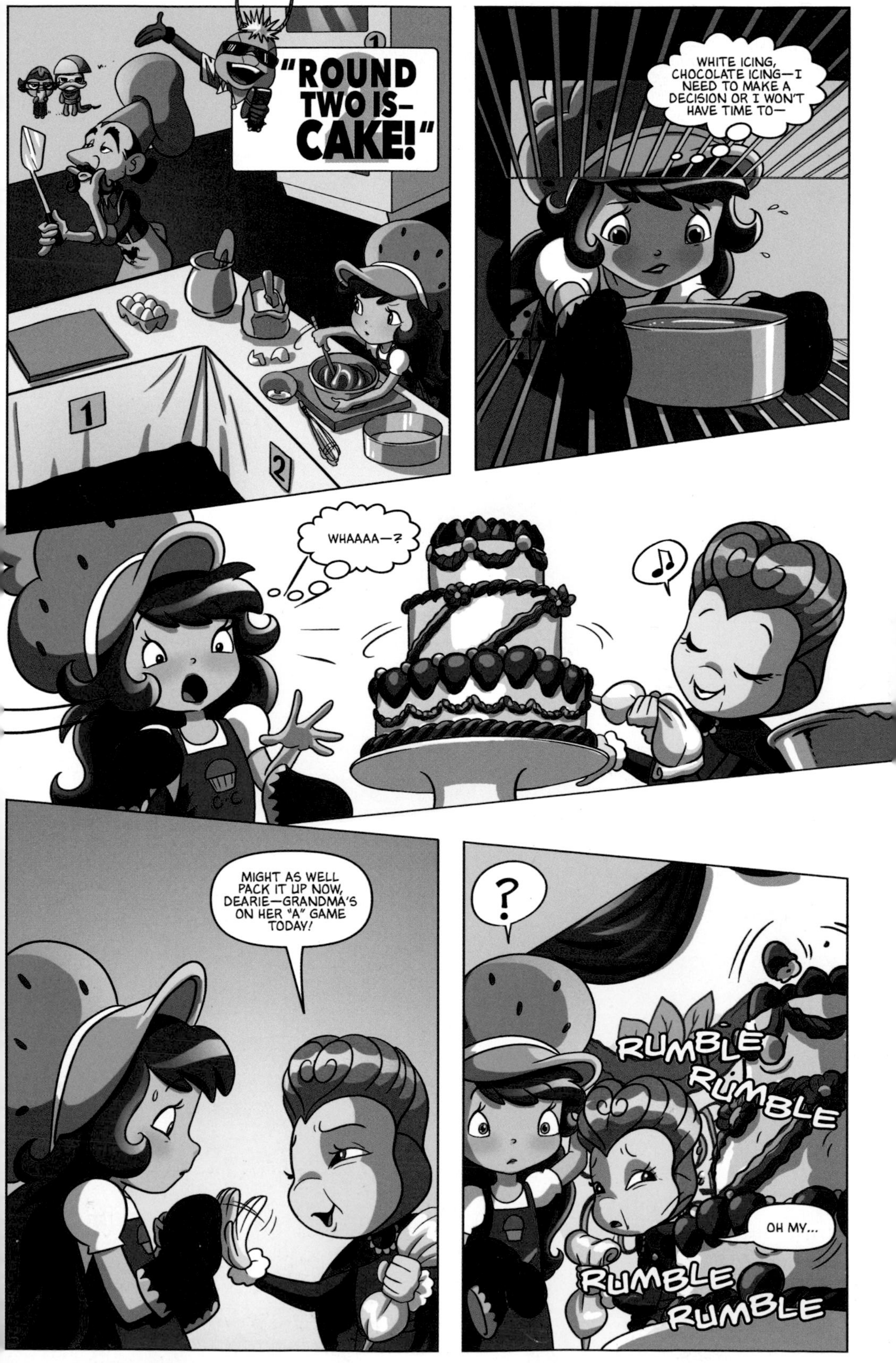
"ROUND TWO IS– CAKE!"
WHITE ICING, CHOCOLATE ICING—I NEED TO MAKE A DECISION OR I WON'T HAVE TIME TO—
WHAAAA—?
♪
MIGHT AS WELL PACK IT UP NOW, DEARIE—GRANDMA'S ON HER "A" GAME TODAY!
?
RUMBLE RUMBLE
OH MY...
RUMBLE RUMBLE

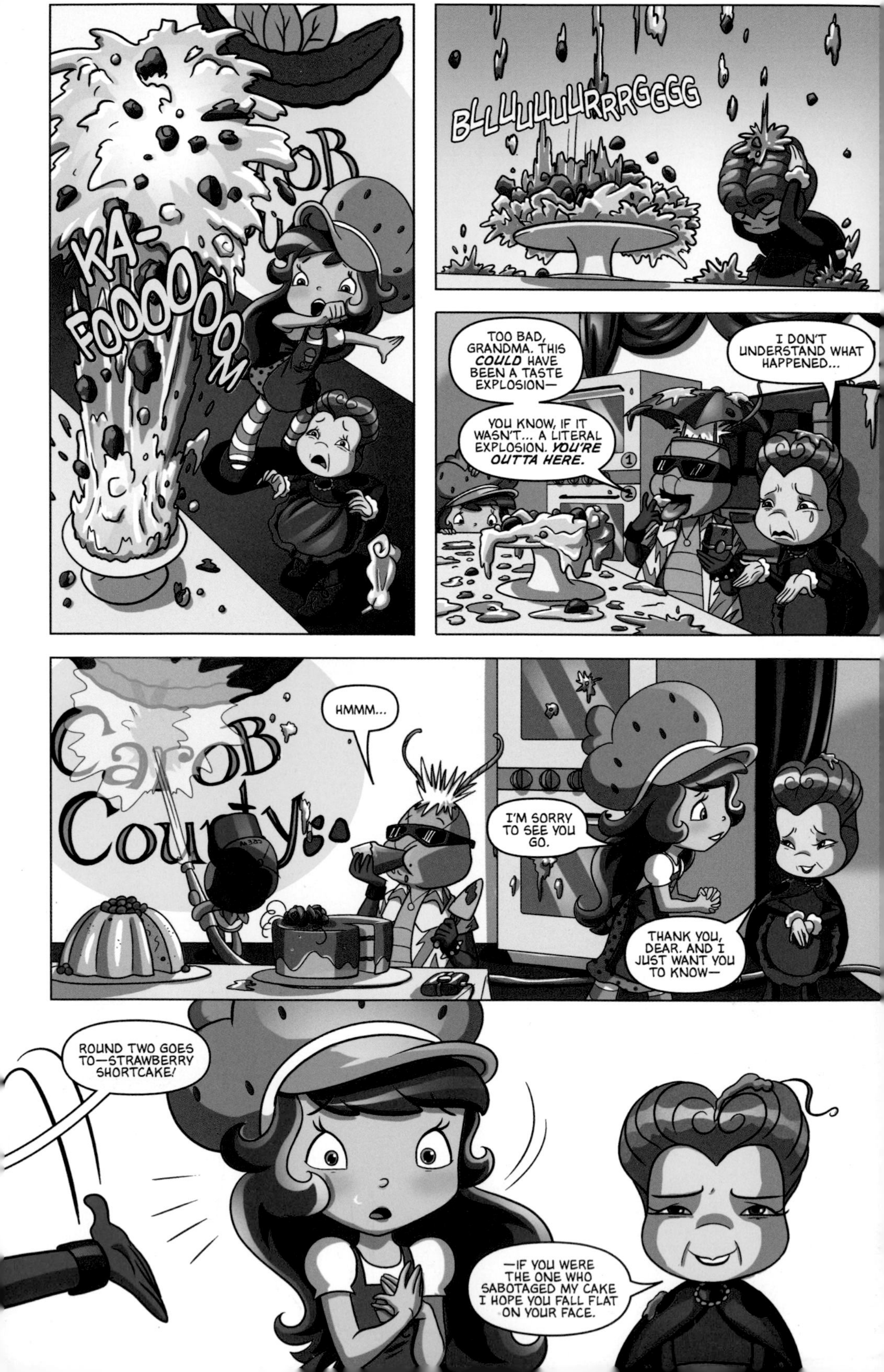
KA-FOOOOOOM
BLLUUUUURRRGGGG
TOO BAD, GRANDMA. THIS *COULD* HAVE BEEN A TASTE EXPLOSION—
YOU KNOW, IF IT WASN'T... A LITERAL EXPLOSION. ***YOU'RE OUTTA HERE.***
I DON'T UNDERSTAND WHAT HAPPENED...
HMMM...
I'M SORRY TO SEE YOU GO.
THANK YOU, DEAR. AND I JUST WANT YOU TO KNOW—
ROUND TWO GOES TO—STRAWBERRY SHORTCAKE!
—IF YOU WERE THE ONE WHO SABOTAGED MY CAKE I HOPE YOU FALL FLAT ON YOUR FACE.

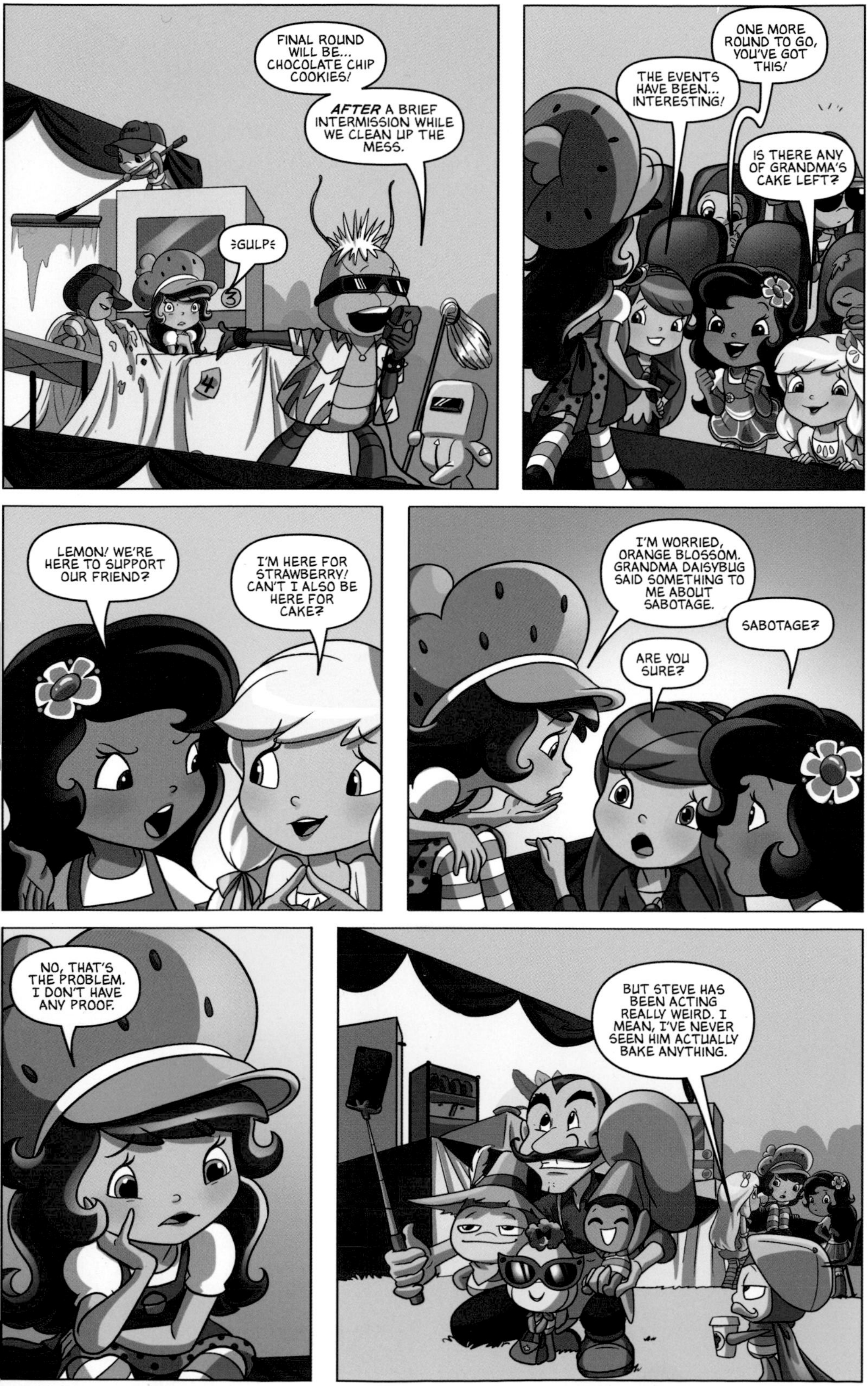
FINAL ROUND WILL BE... CHOCOLATE CHIP COOKIES!
AFTER A BRIEF INTERMISSION WHILE WE CLEAN UP THE MESS.
GULP
THE EVENTS HAVE BEEN... INTERESTING!
ONE MORE ROUND TO GO, YOU'VE GOT THIS!
IS THERE ANY OF GRANDMA'S CAKE LEFT?
LEMON! WE'RE HERE TO SUPPORT OUR FRIEND!
I'M HERE FOR STRAWBERRY! CAN'T I ALSO BE HERE FOR CAKE?
I'M WORRIED, ORANGE BLOSSOM. GRANDMA DAISYBUG SAID SOMETHING TO ME ABOUT SABOTAGE.
ARE YOU SURE?
SABOTAGE?
NO, THAT'S THE PROBLEM. I DON'T HAVE ANY PROOF.
BUT STEVE HAS BEEN ACTING REALLY WEIRD. I MEAN, I'VE NEVER SEEN HIM ACTUALLY BAKE ANYTHING.

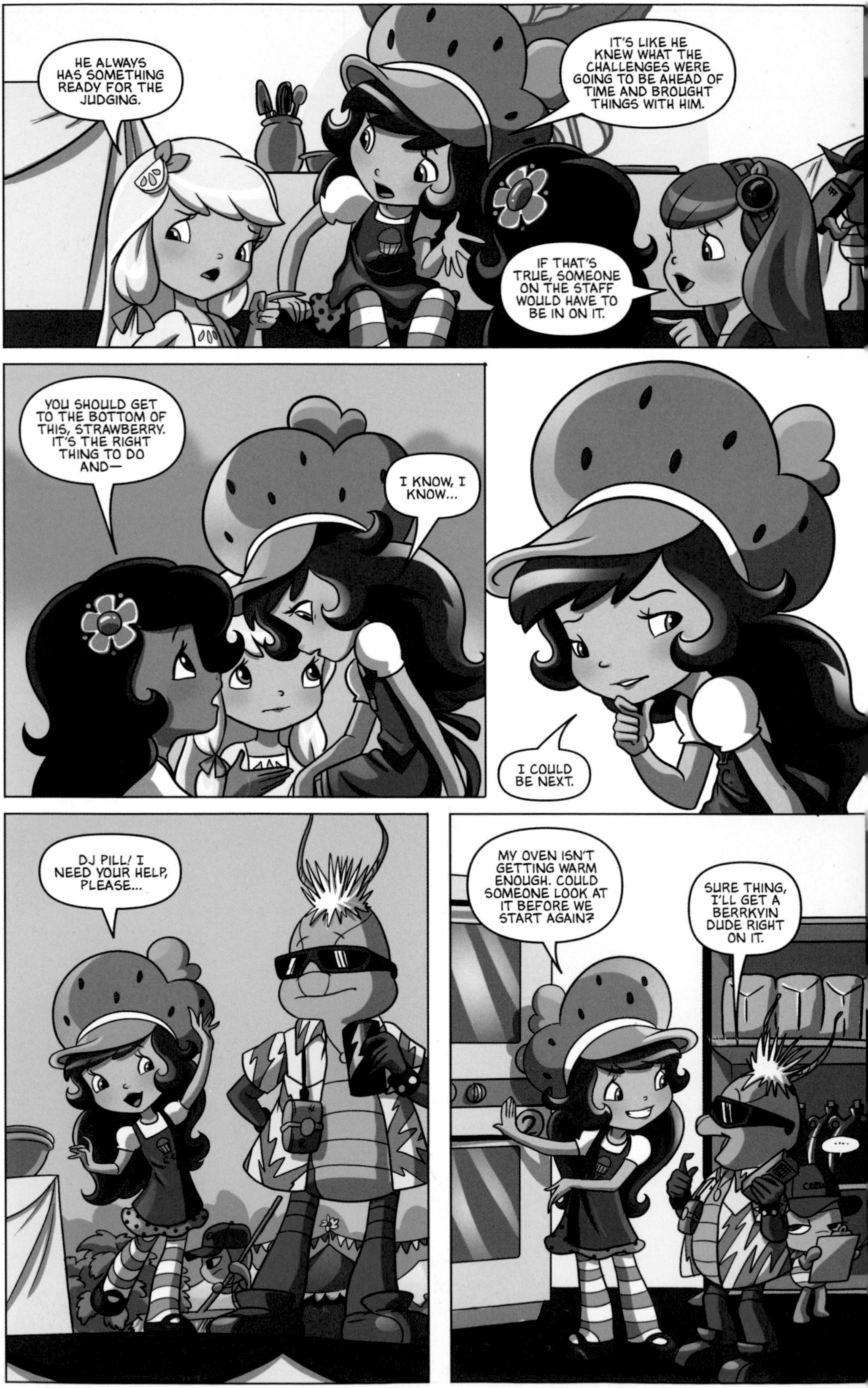
HE ALWAYS HAS SOMETHING READY FOR THE JUDGING.
IT'S LIKE HE KNEW WHAT THE CHALLENGES WERE GOING TO BE AHEAD OF TIME AND BROUGHT THINGS WITH HIM.
IF THAT'S TRUE, SOMEONE ON THE STAFF WOULD HAVE TO BE IN ON IT.
YOU SHOULD GET TO THE BOTTOM OF THIS, STRAWBERRY. IT'S THE RIGHT THING TO DO AND—
I KNOW, I KNOW...
I COULD BE NEXT.
DJ PILL! I NEED YOUR HELP, PLEASE...
MY OVEN ISN'T GETTING WARM ENOUGH. COULD SOMEONE LOOK AT IT BEFORE WE START AGAIN?
SURE THING, I'LL GET A BERRKYIN DUDE RIGHT ON IT.

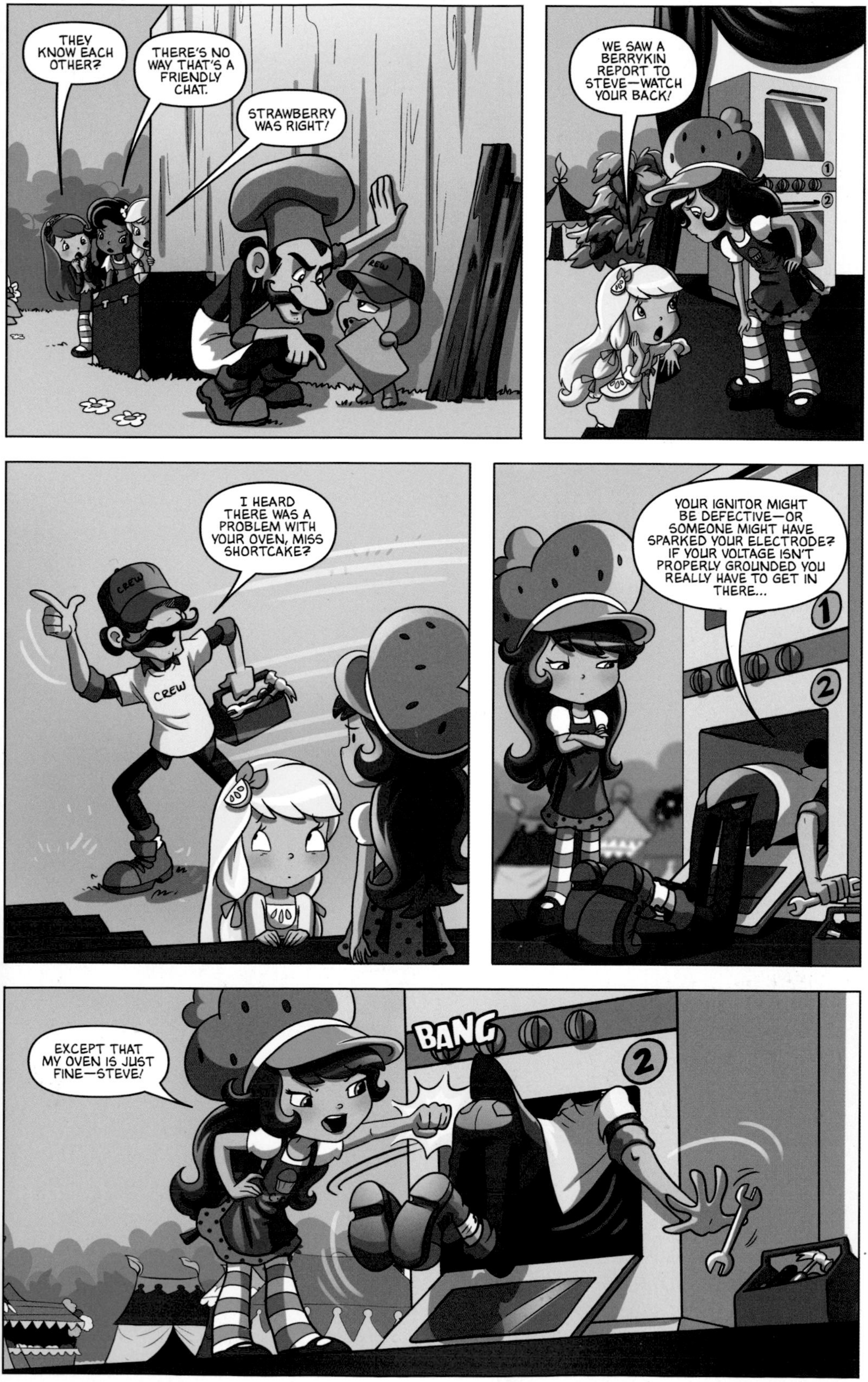
THEY KNOW EACH OTHER?
THERE'S NO WAY THAT'S A FRIENDLY CHAT.
STRAWBERRY WAS RIGHT!
CREW
WE SAW A BERRYKIN REPORT TO STEVE—WATCH YOUR BACK!
1
2
I HEARD THERE WAS A PROBLEM WITH YOUR OVEN, MISS SHORTCAKE?
CREW
CREW
YOUR IGNITOR MIGHT BE DEFECTIVE—OR SOMEONE MIGHT HAVE SPARKED YOUR ELECTRODE? IF YOUR VOLTAGE ISN'T PROPERLY GROUNDED YOU REALLY HAVE TO GET IN THERE...
1
2
EXCEPT THAT MY OVEN IS JUST FINE—STEVE!
BANG
2

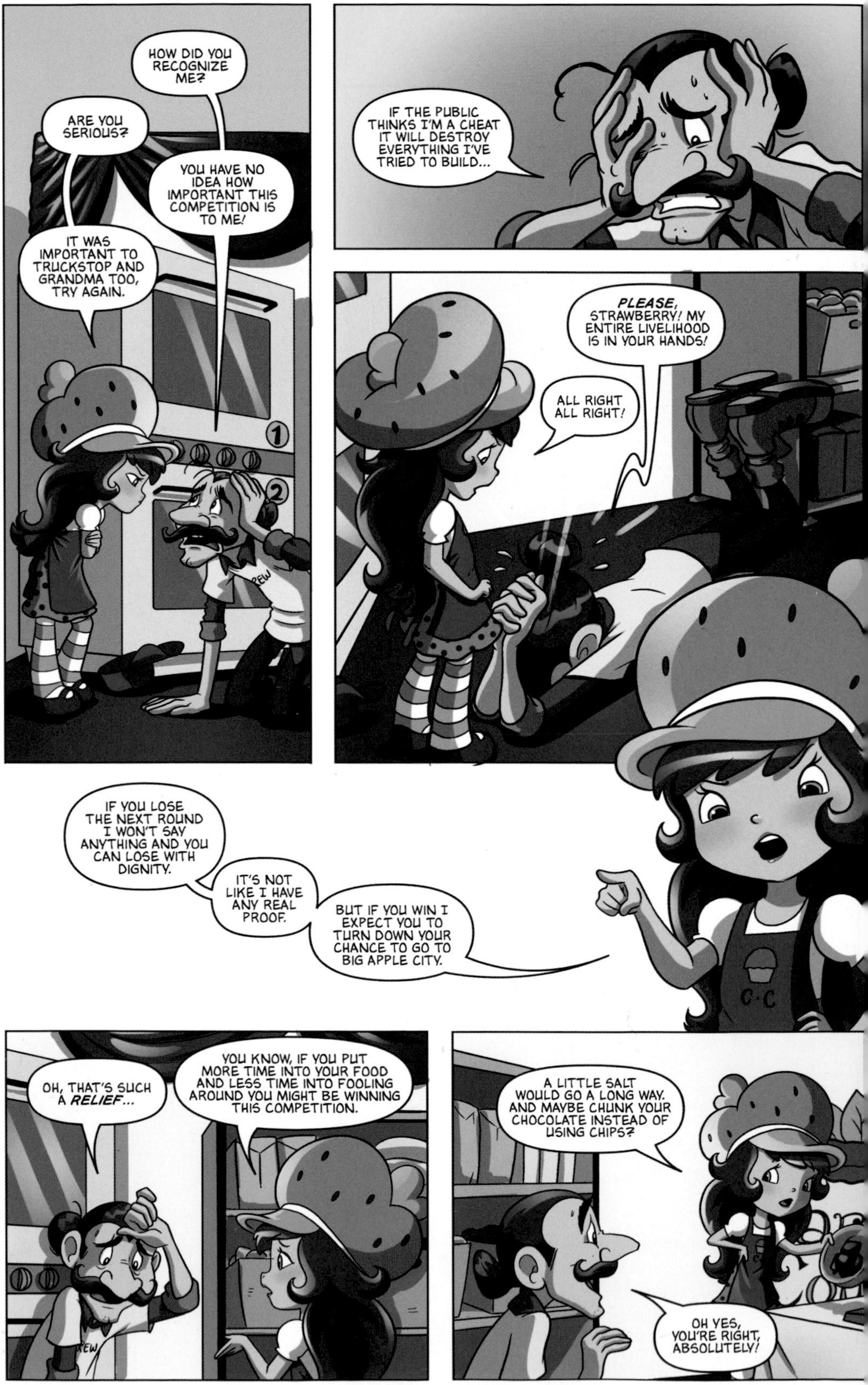
HOW DID YOU RECOGNIZE ME?
ARE YOU SERIOUS?
YOU HAVE NO IDEA HOW IMPORTANT THIS COMPETITION IS TO ME!
IT WAS IMPORTANT TO TRUCKSTOP AND GRANDMA TOO, TRY AGAIN.
IF THE PUBLIC THINKS I'M A CHEAT IT WILL DESTROY EVERYTHING I'VE TRIED TO BUILD...
PLEASE, STRAWBERRY! MY ENTIRE LIVELIHOOD IS IN YOUR HANDS!
ALL RIGHT ALL RIGHT!
IF YOU LOSE THE NEXT ROUND I WON'T SAY ANYTHING AND YOU CAN LOSE WITH DIGNITY.
IT'S NOT LIKE I HAVE ANY REAL PROOF.
BUT IF YOU WIN I EXPECT YOU TO TURN DOWN YOUR CHANCE TO GO TO BIG APPLE CITY.
OH, THAT'S SUCH A RELIEF...
YOU KNOW, IF YOU PUT MORE TIME INTO YOUR FOOD AND LESS TIME INTO FOOLING AROUND YOU MIGHT BE WINNING THIS COMPETITION.
A LITTLE SALT WOULD GO A LONG WAY. AND MAYBE CHUNK YOUR CHOCOLATE INSTEAD OF USING CHIPS?
OH YES, YOU'RE RIGHT, ABSOLUTELY!

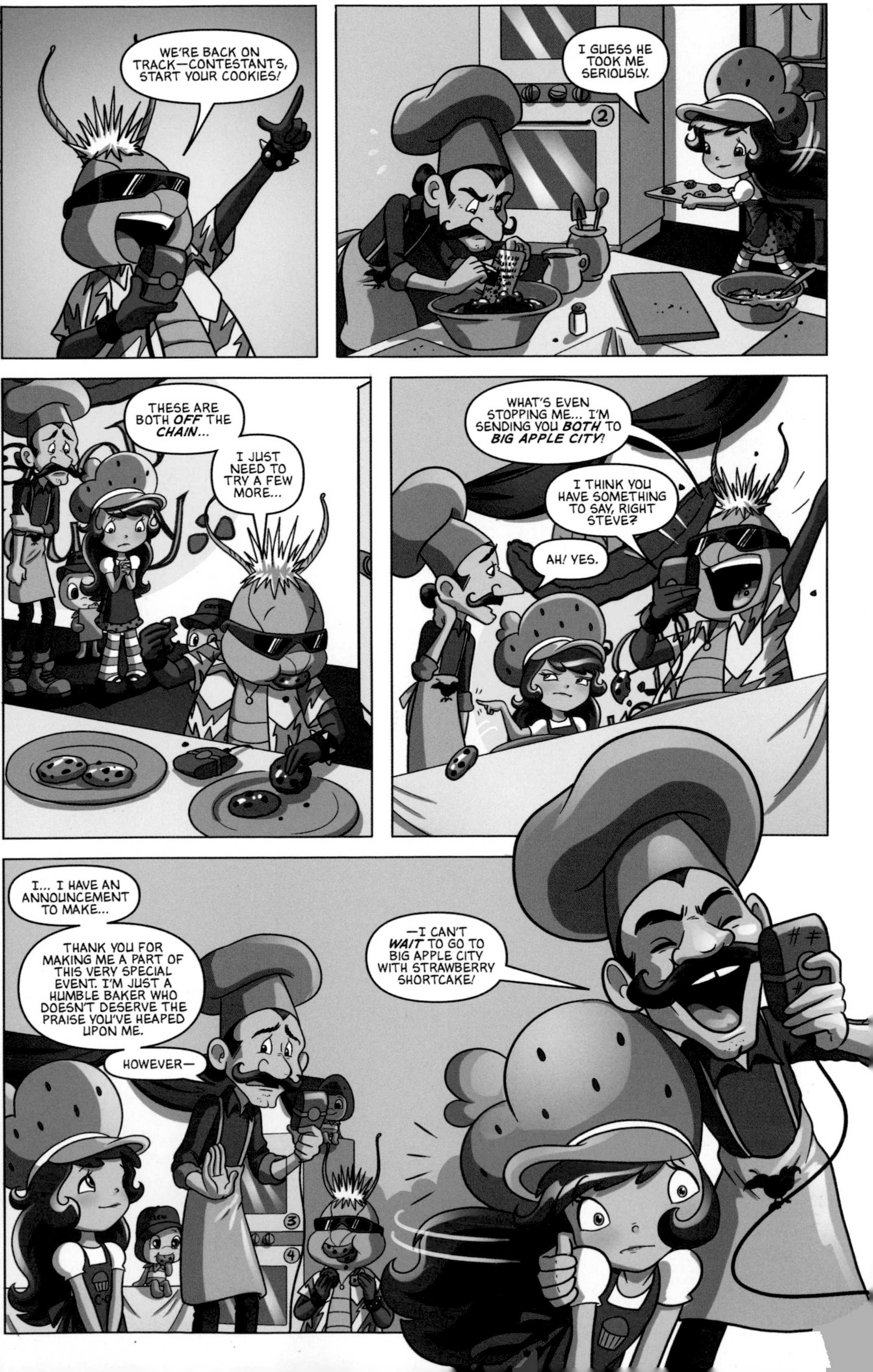
WE'RE BACK ON TRACK—CONTESTANTS, START YOUR COOKIES!
I GUESS HE TOOK ME SERIOUSLY.
2
THESE ARE BOTH *OFF* THE *CHAIN*...
I JUST NEED TO TRY A FEW MORE...
WHAT'S EVEN STOPPING ME... I'M SENDING YOU *BOTH* TO *BIG APPLE CITY*!
I THINK YOU HAVE SOMETHING TO SAY, RIGHT STEVE?
AH! YES.
I... I HAVE AN ANNOUNCEMENT TO MAKE...
THANK YOU FOR MAKING ME A PART OF THIS VERY SPECIAL EVENT. I'M JUST A HUMBLE BAKER WHO DOESN'T DESERVE THE PRAISE YOU'VE HEAPED UPON ME.
HOWEVER—
—I CAN'T *WAIT* TO GO TO BIG APPLE CITY WITH STRAWBERRY SHORTCAKE!
3
4

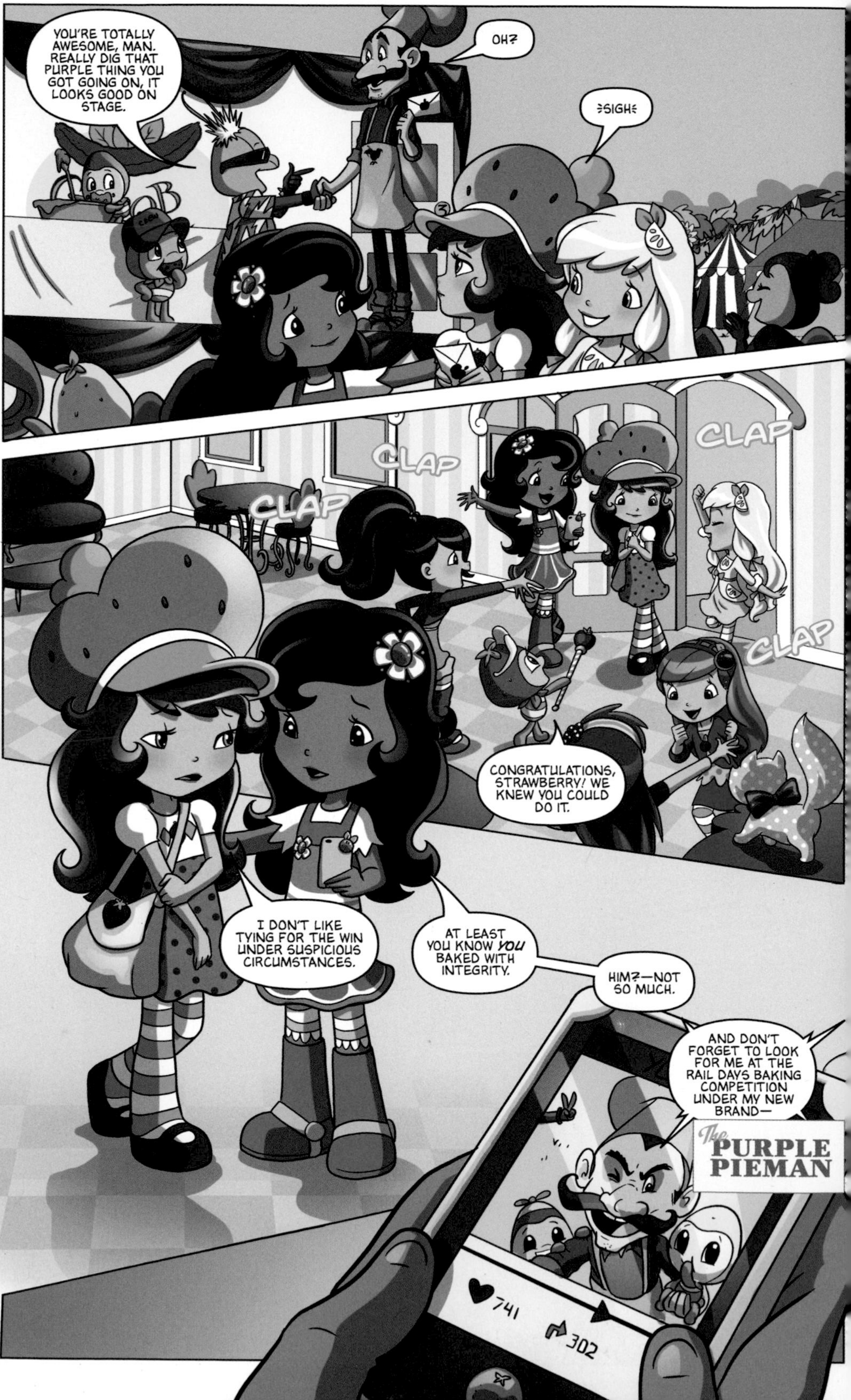
YOU'RE TOTALLY AWESOME, MAN. REALLY DIG THAT PURPLE THING YOU GOT GOING ON, IT LOOKS GOOD ON STAGE.
OH?
SIGH
CLAP
CLAP
CLAP
CLAP
CONGRATULATIONS, STRAWBERRY! WE KNEW YOU COULD DO IT.
I DON'T LIKE TYING FOR THE WIN UNDER SUSPICIOUS CIRCUMSTANCES.
AT LEAST YOU KNOW *YOU* BAKED WITH INTEGRITY.
HIM?—NOT SO MUCH.
AND DON'T FORGET TO LOOK FOR ME AT THE RAIL DAYS BAKING COMPETITION UNDER MY NEW BRAND—
The PURPLE PIEMAN
741
302

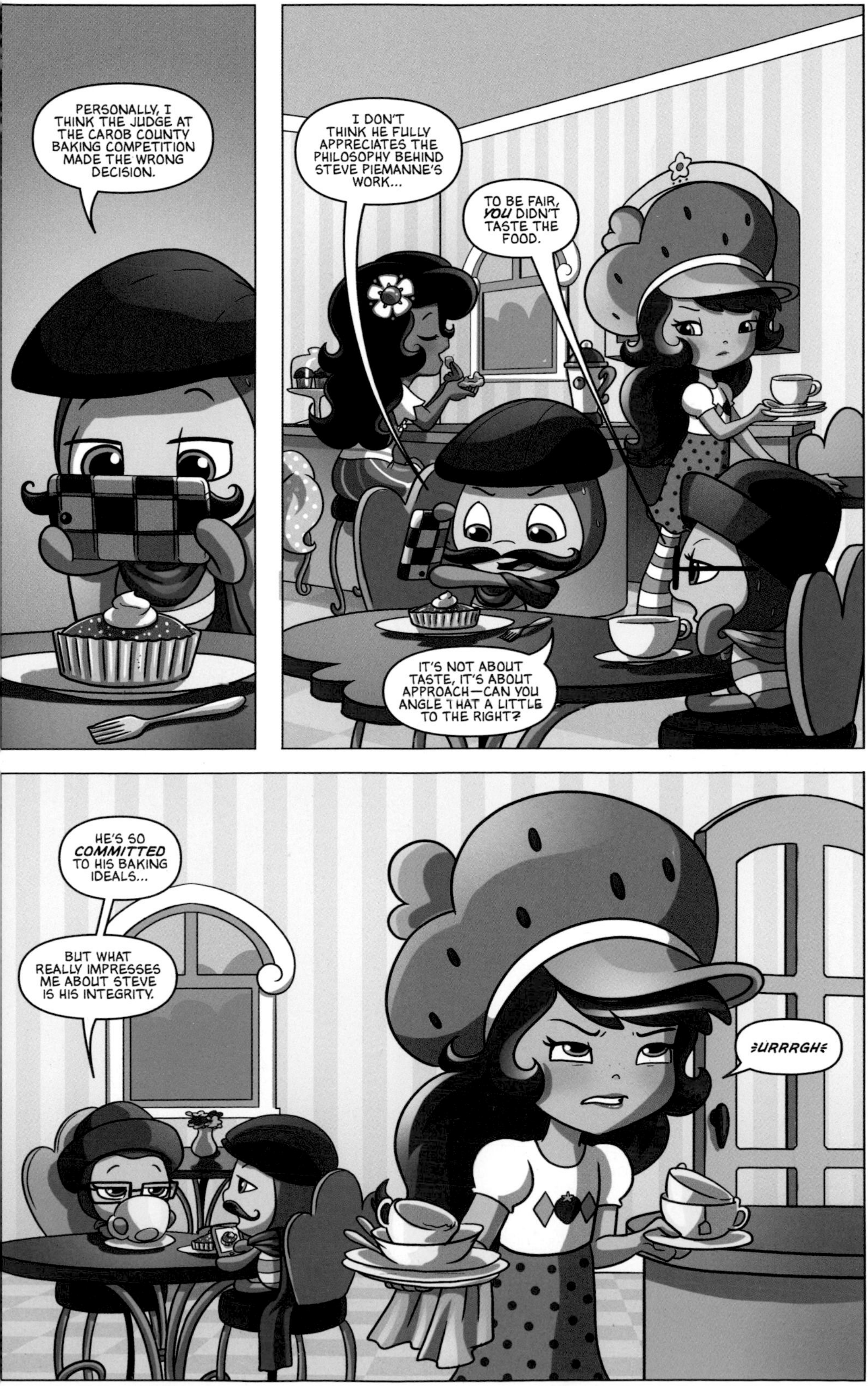
PERSONALLY, I THINK THE JUDGE AT THE CAROB COUNTY BAKING COMPETITION MADE THE WRONG DECISION.
I DON'T THINK HE FULLY APPRECIATES THE PHILOSOPHY BEHIND STEVE PIEMANNE'S WORK...
TO BE FAIR, *YOU* DIDN'T TASTE THE FOOD.
IT'S NOT ABOUT TASTE, IT'S ABOUT APPROACH—CAN YOU ANGLE THAT A LITTLE TO THE RIGHT?
HE'S SO ***COMMITTED*** TO HIS BAKING IDEALS...
BUT WHAT REALLY IMPRESSES ME ABOUT STEVE IS HIS INTEGRITY.
URRRGH

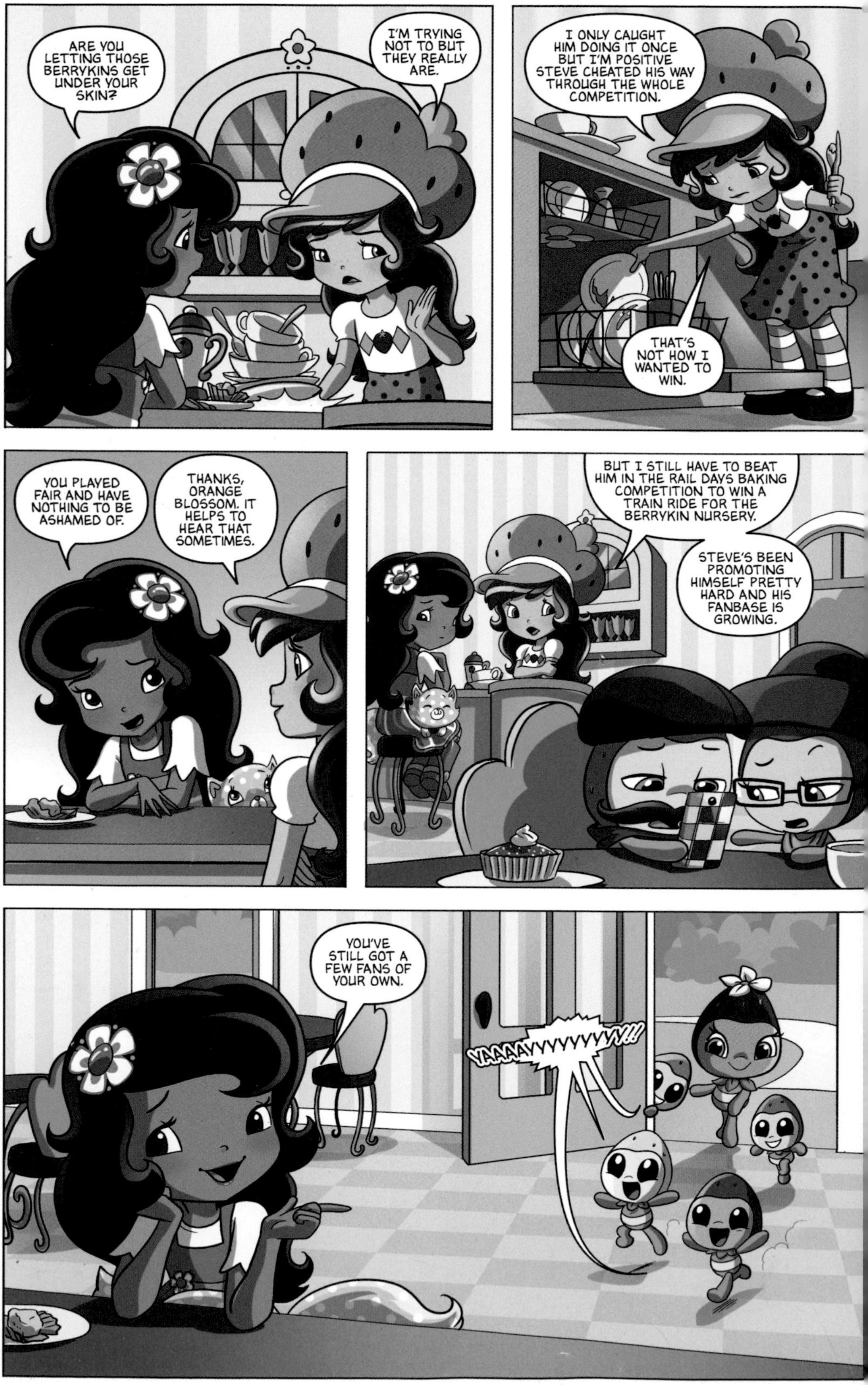
ARE YOU LETTING THOSE BERRYKINS GET UNDER YOUR SKIN?
I'M TRYING NOT TO BUT THEY REALLY ARE.
I ONLY CAUGHT HIM DOING IT ONCE BUT I'M POSITIVE STEVE CHEATED HIS WAY THROUGH THE WHOLE COMPETITION.
THAT'S NOT HOW I WANTED TO WIN.
YOU PLAYED FAIR AND HAVE NOTHING TO BE ASHAMED OF.
THANKS, ORANGE BLOSSOM. IT HELPS TO HEAR THAT SOMETIMES.
BUT I STILL HAVE TO BEAT HIM IN THE RAIL DAYS BAKING COMPETITION TO WIN A TRAIN RIDE FOR THE BERRYKIN NURSERY.
STEVE'S BEEN PROMOTING HIMSELF PRETTY HARD AND HIS FANBASE IS GROWING.
YOU'VE STILL GOT A FEW FANS OF YOUR OWN.
YAAAAYYYYYYYYY!!

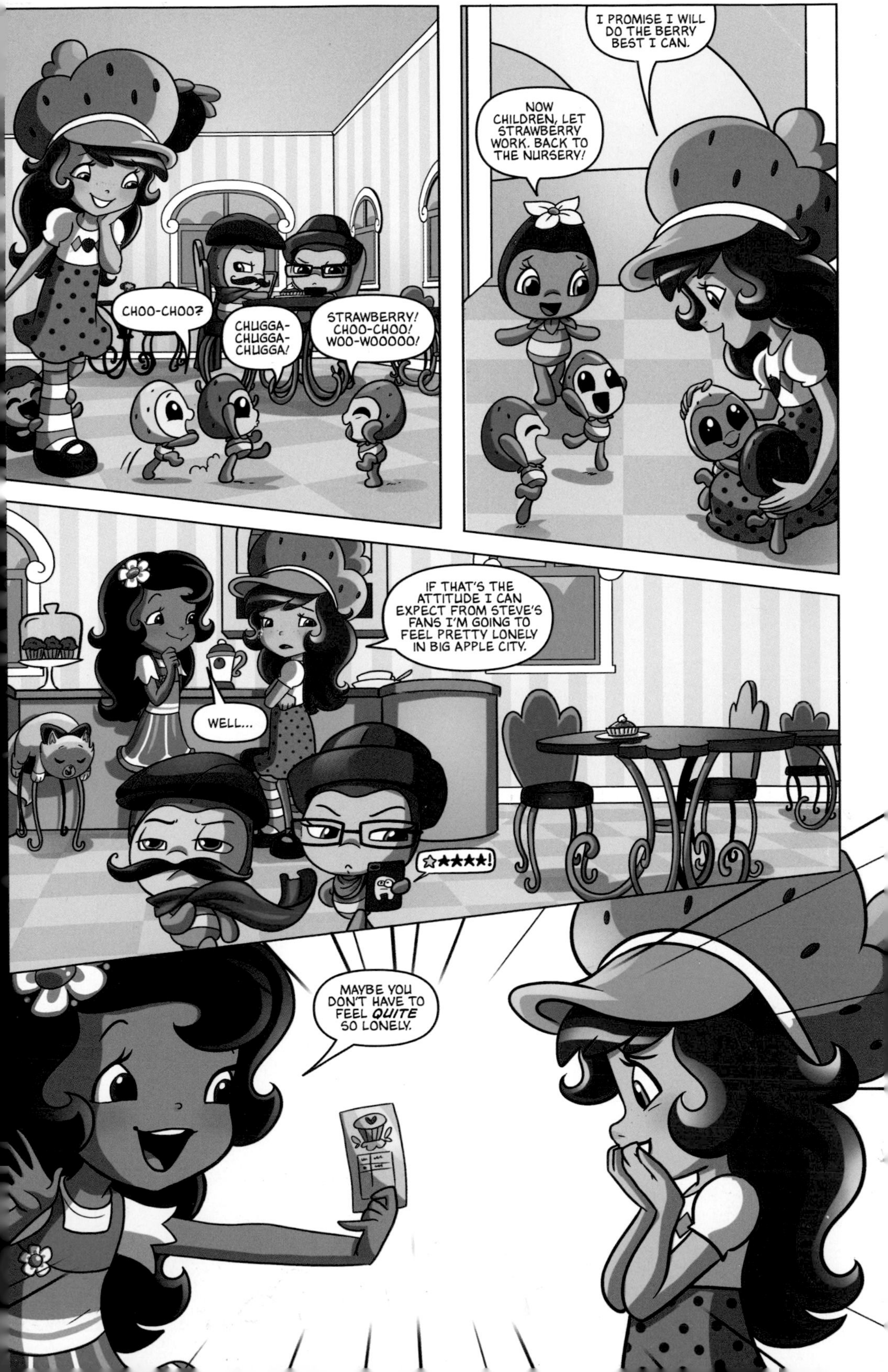
CHOO-CHOO?
CHUGGA-CHUGGA-CHUGGA!
STRAWBERRY! CHOO-CHOO! WOO-WOOOOO!
I PROMISE I WILL DO THE BERRY BEST I CAN.
NOW CHILDREN, LET STRAWBERRY WORK. BACK TO THE NURSERY!
IF THAT'S THE ATTITUDE I CAN EXPECT FROM STEVE'S FANS I'M GOING TO FEEL PRETTY LONELY IN BIG APPLE CITY.
WELL...
☆★★★★!
MAYBE YOU DON'T HAVE TO FEEL *QUITE* SO LONELY.

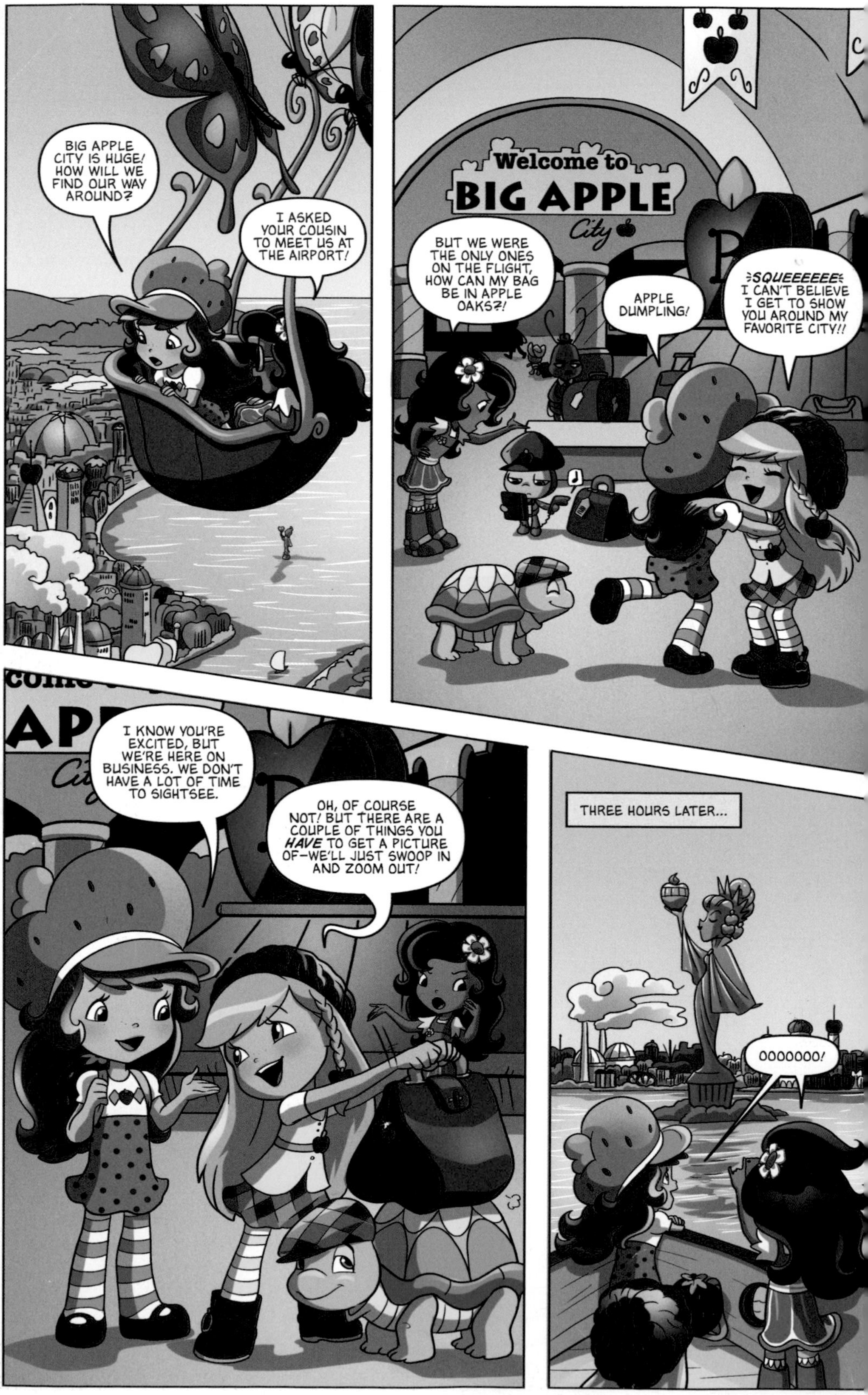
BIG APPLE CITY IS HUGE! HOW WILL WE FIND OUR WAY AROUND?
I ASKED YOUR COUSIN TO MEET US AT THE AIRPORT!
Welcome to BIG APPLE City
BUT WE WERE THE ONLY ONES ON THE FLIGHT, HOW CAN MY BAG BE IN APPLE OAKS?!
APPLE DUMPLING!
SQUEEEEEE! I CAN'T BELIEVE I GET TO SHOW YOU AROUND MY FAVORITE CITY!!
I KNOW YOU'RE EXCITED, BUT WE'RE HERE ON BUSINESS. WE DON'T HAVE A LOT OF TIME TO SIGHTSEE.
OH, OF COURSE NOT! BUT THERE ARE A COUPLE OF THINGS YOU HAVE TO GET A PICTURE OF—WE'LL JUST SWOOP IN AND ZOOM OUT!
THREE HOURS LATER...
OOOOOOO!

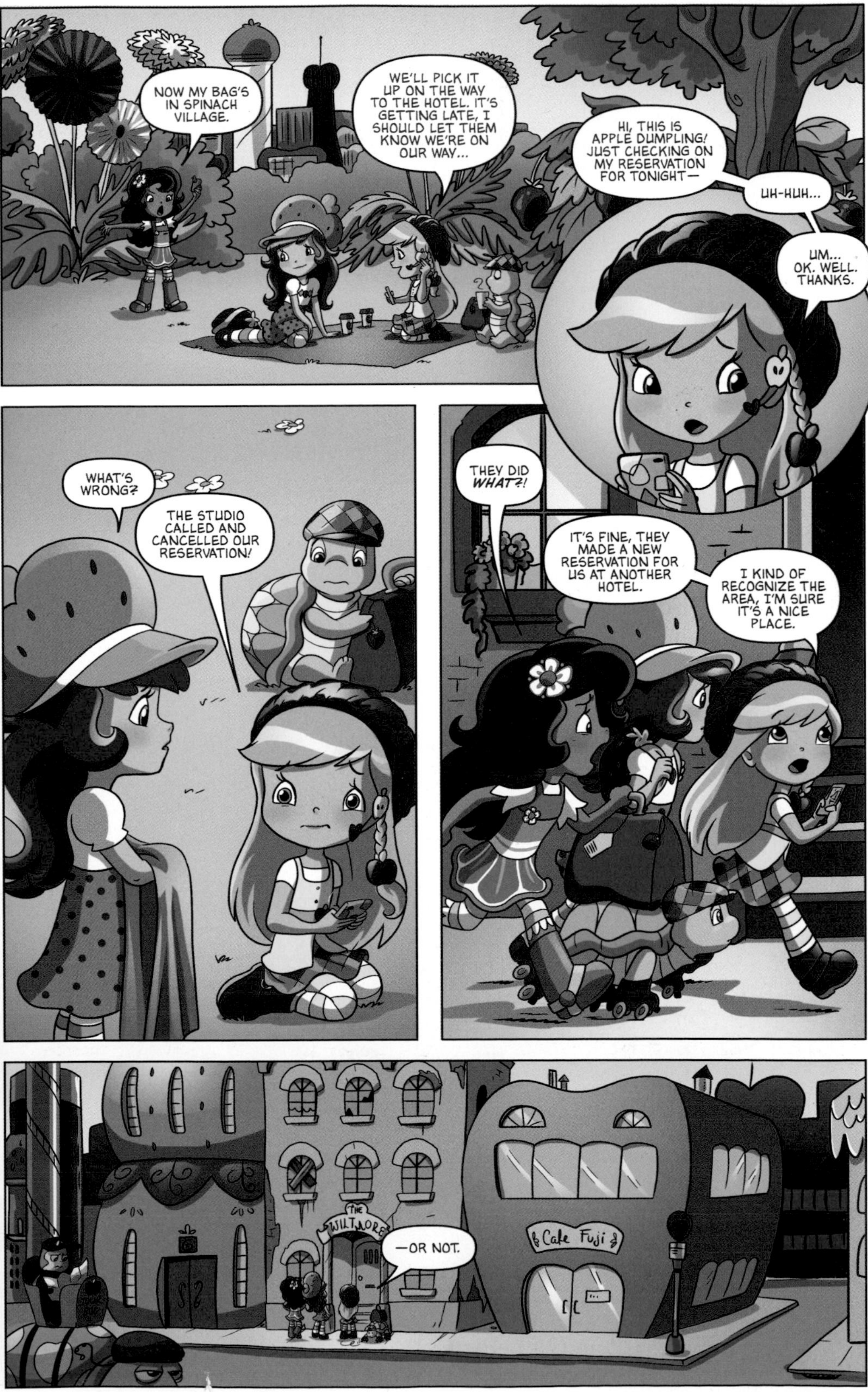
NOW MY BAG'S IN SPINACH VILLAGE.
WE'LL PICK IT UP ON THE WAY TO THE HOTEL. IT'S GETTING LATE, I SHOULD LET THEM KNOW WE'RE ON OUR WAY...
HI, THIS IS APPLE DUMPLING! JUST CHECKING ON MY RESERVATION FOR TONIGHT—
UH-HUH...
UM... OK. WELL. THANKS.
WHAT'S WRONG?
THE STUDIO CALLED AND CANCELLED OUR RESERVATION!
THEY DID WHAT?!
IT'S FINE, THEY MADE A NEW RESERVATION FOR US AT ANOTHER HOTEL.
I KIND OF RECOGNIZE THE AREA, I'M SURE IT'S A NICE PLACE.
—OR NOT.
Cafe Fuji

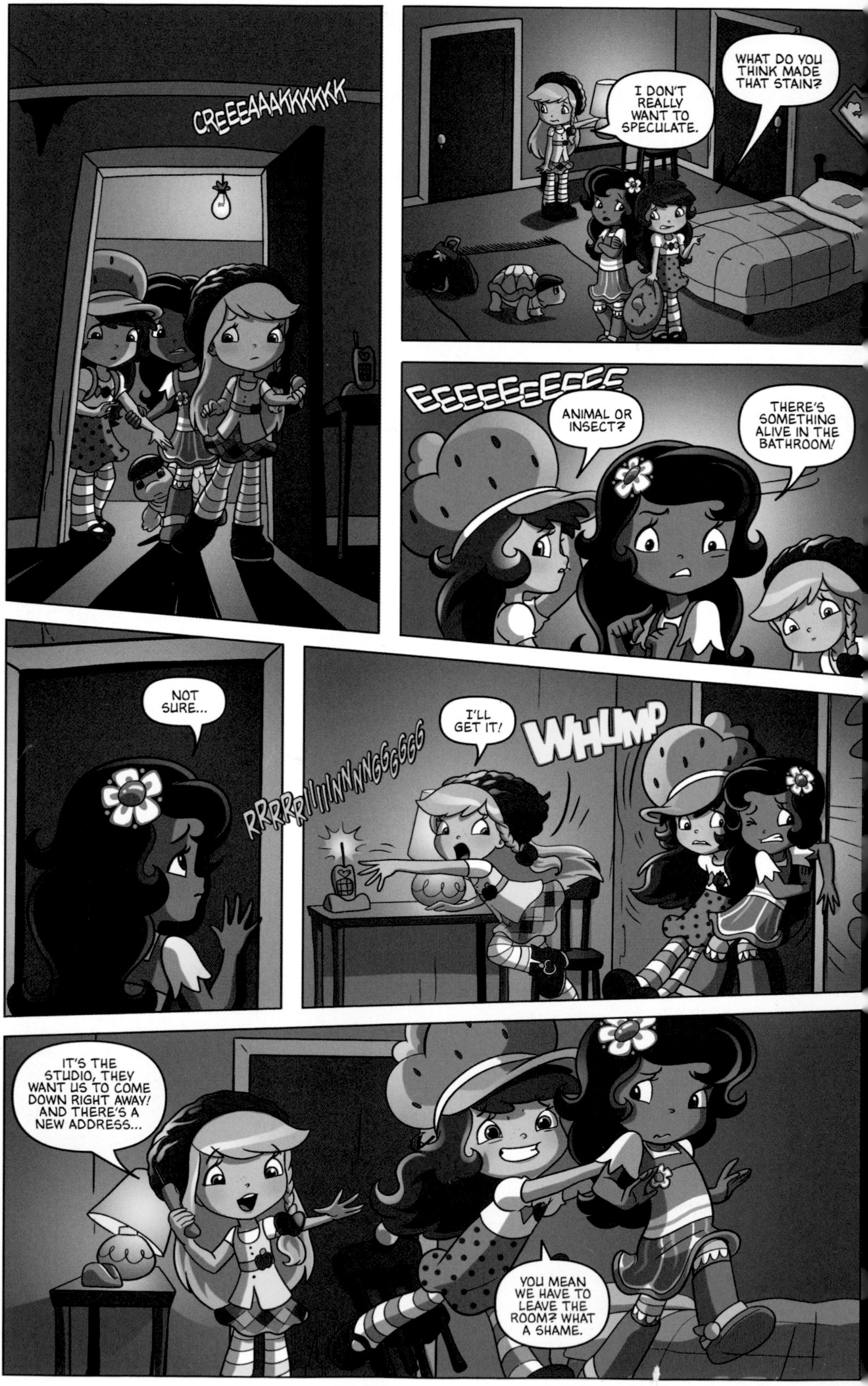
CREEEAAAKKKKKK
I DON'T REALLY WANT TO SPECULATE.
WHAT DO YOU THINK MADE THAT STAIN?
EEEEEEEEEEE
ANIMAL OR INSECT?
THERE'S SOMETHING ALIVE IN THE BATHROOM!
NOT SURE...
RRRRRIIIIINNNNGGGGGG
I'LL GET IT!
WHUMP
IT'S THE STUDIO, THEY WANT US TO COME DOWN RIGHT AWAY! AND THERE'S A NEW ADDRESS...
YOU MEAN WE HAVE TO LEAVE THE ROOM? WHAT A SHAME.

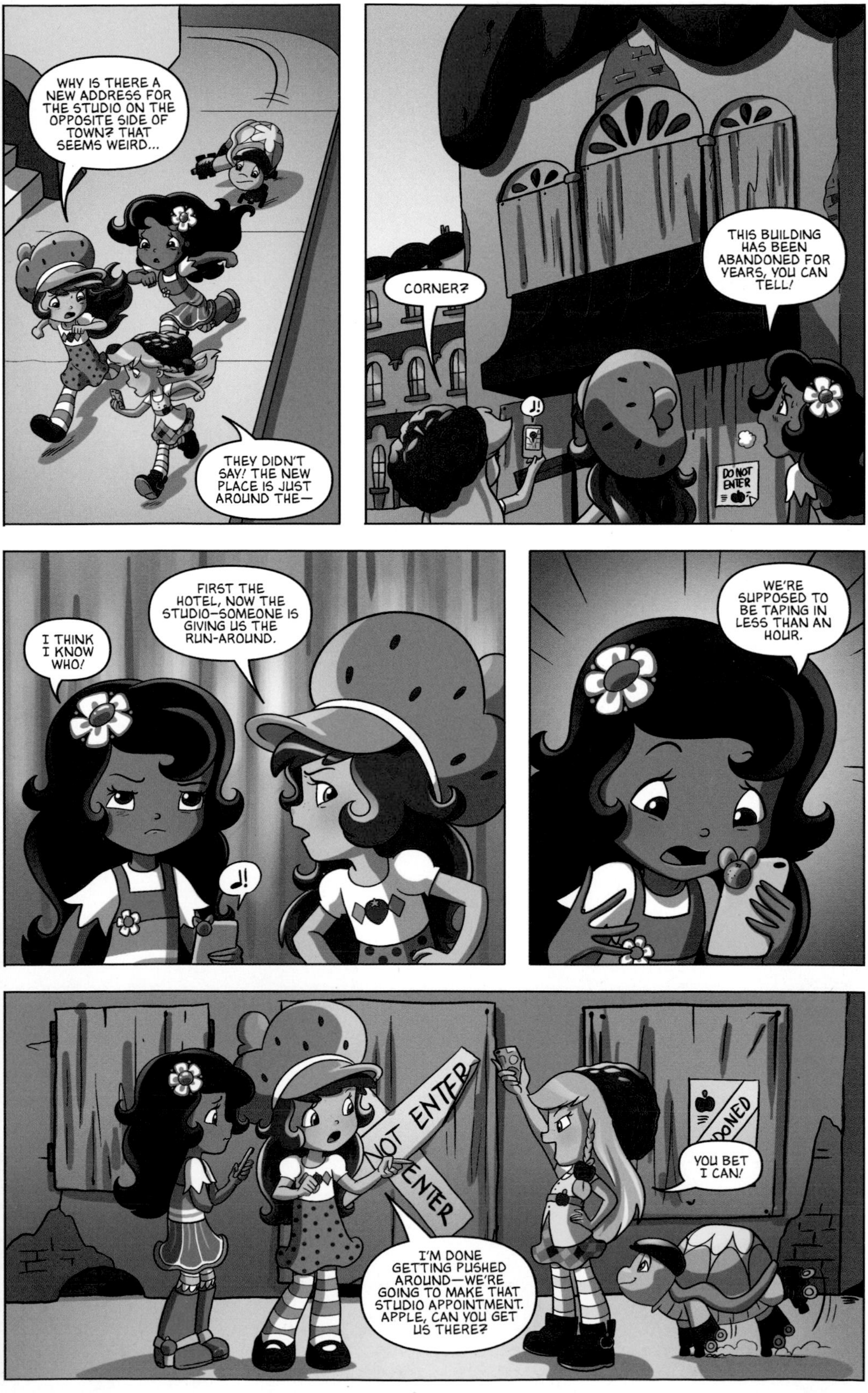
WHY IS THERE A NEW ADDRESS FOR THE STUDIO ON THE OPPOSITE SIDE OF TOWN? THAT SEEMS WEIRD...
THEY DIDN'T SAY! THE NEW PLACE IS JUST AROUND THE—
CORNER?
♩!
THIS BUILDING HAS BEEN ABANDONED FOR YEARS, YOU CAN TELL!
DO NOT ENTER
I THINK I KNOW WHO!
FIRST THE HOTEL, NOW THE STUDIO—SOMEONE IS GIVING US THE RUN-AROUND.
♩!
WE'RE SUPPOSED TO BE TAPING IN LESS THAN AN HOUR.
NOT ENTER
ENTER
DONED
YOU BET I CAN!
I'M DONE GETTING PUSHED AROUND—WE'RE GOING TO MAKE THAT STUDIO APPOINTMENT. APPLE, CAN YOU GET US THERE?

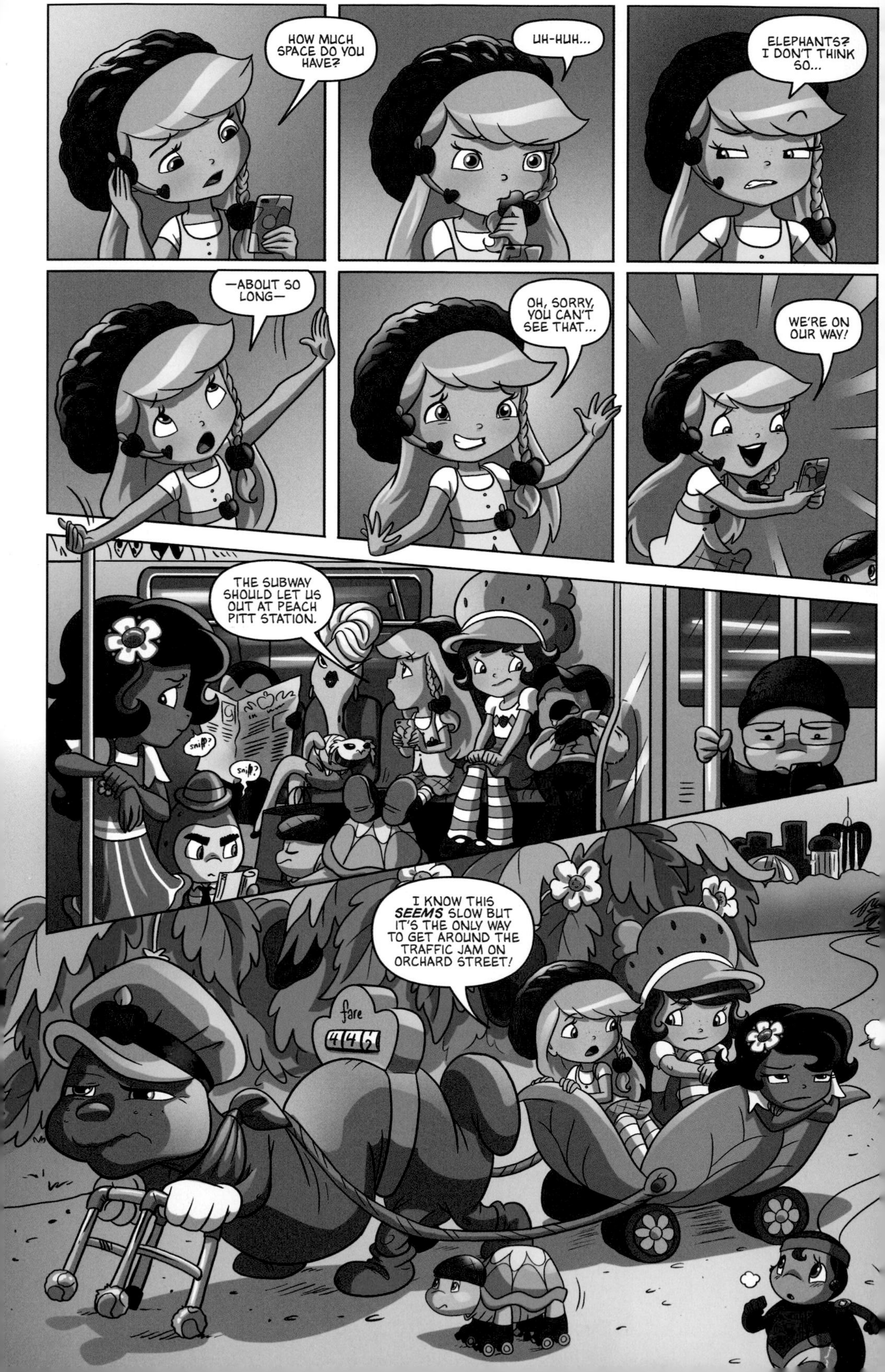
HOW MUCH SPACE DO YOU HAVE?
UH-HUH...
ELEPHANTS? I DON'T THINK SO...
—ABOUT SO LONG—
OH, SORRY, YOU CAN'T SEE THAT...
WE'RE ON OUR WAY!
THE SUBWAY SHOULD LET US OUT AT PEACH PITT STATION.
I KNOW THIS *SEEMS* SLOW BUT IT'S THE ONLY WAY TO GET AROUND THE TRAFFIC JAM ON ORCHARD STREET!
fare

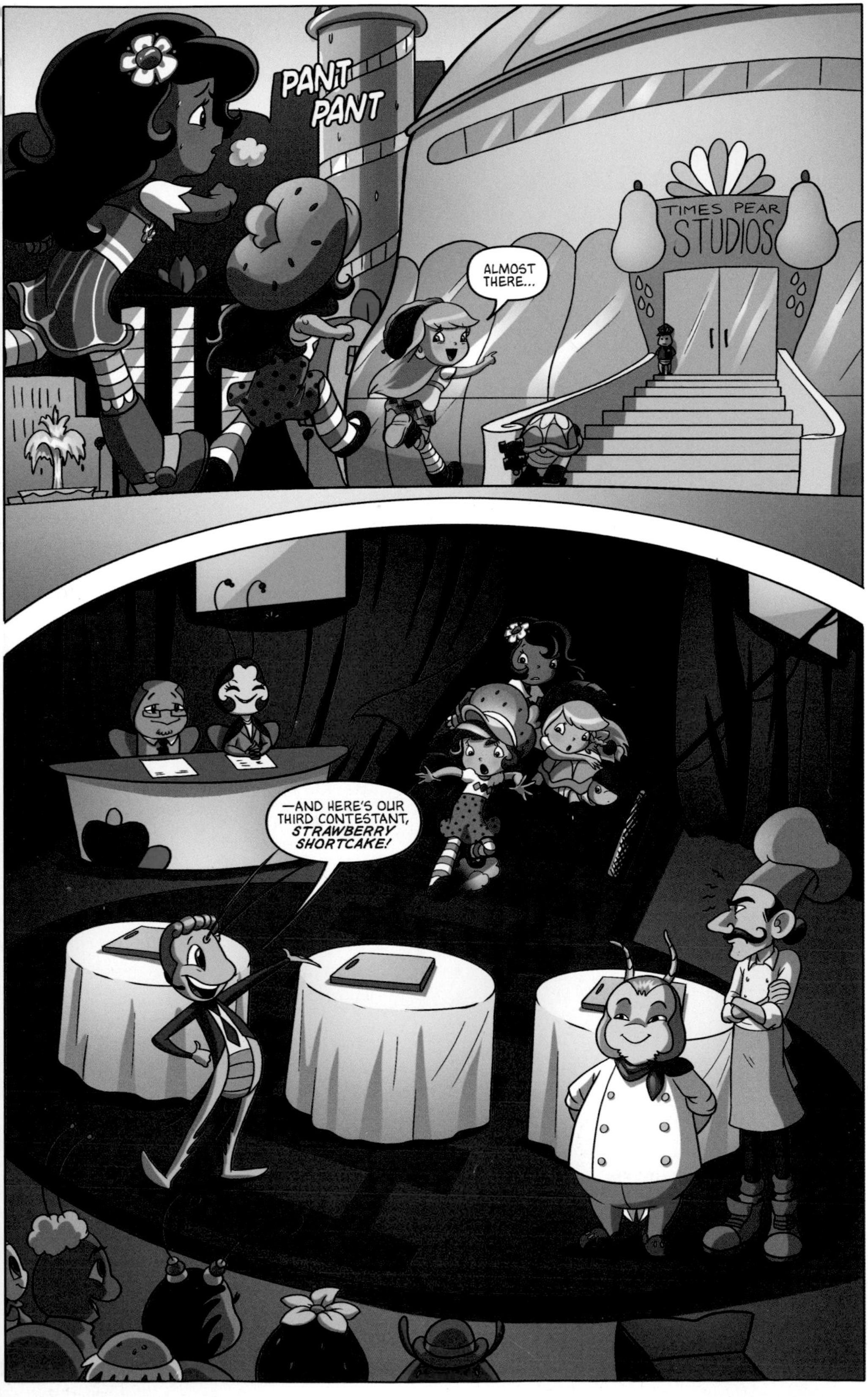
PANT PANT
TIMES PEAR STUDIOS
ALMOST THERE...
—AND HERE'S OUR THIRD CONTESTANT, STRAWBERRY SHORTCAKE!

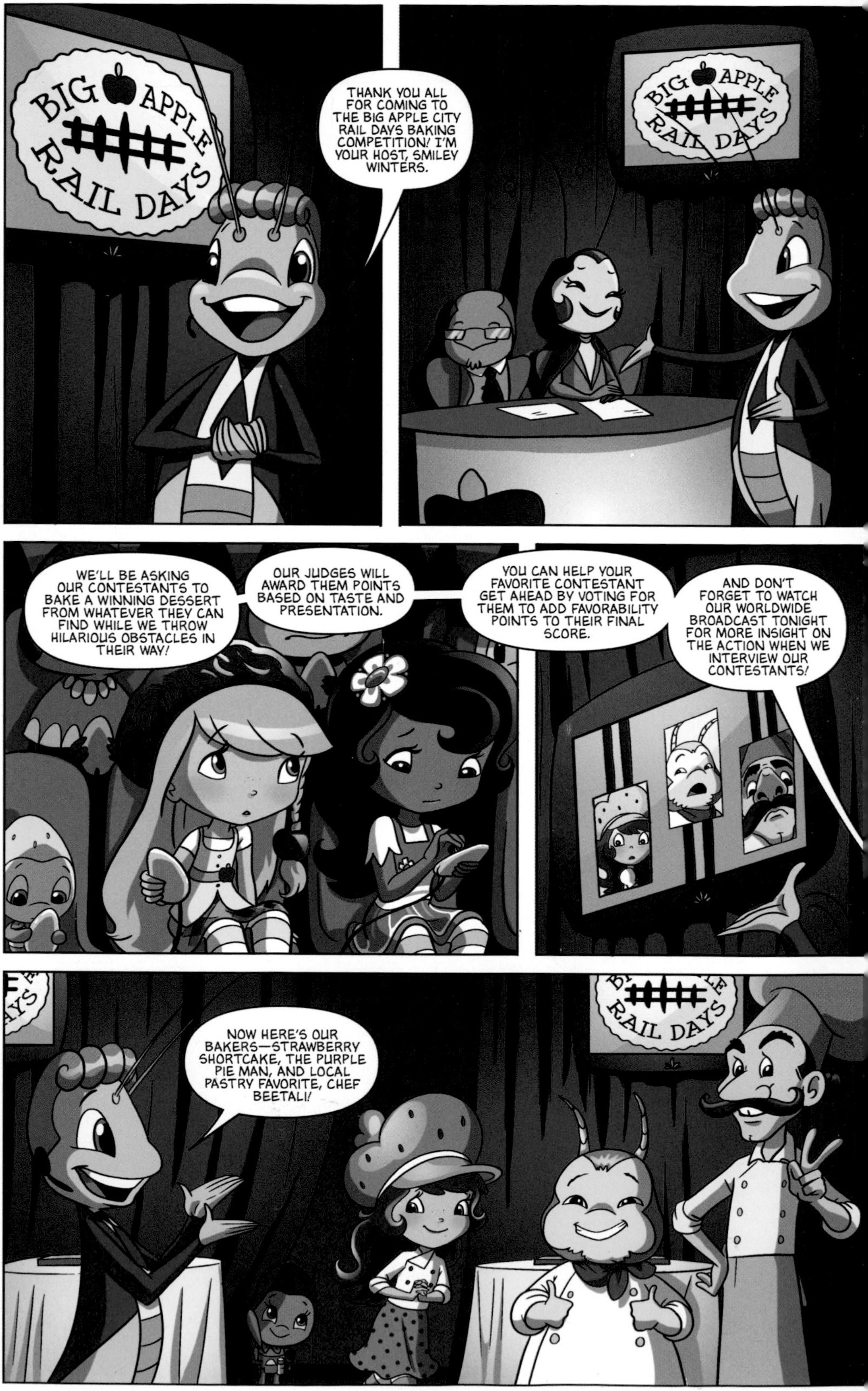
BIG APPLE RAIL DAYS
THANK YOU ALL FOR COMING TO THE BIG APPLE CITY RAIL DAYS BAKING COMPETITION! I'M YOUR HOST, SMILEY WINTERS.
BIG APPLE RAIL DAYS
WE'LL BE ASKING OUR CONTESTANTS TO BAKE A WINNING DESSERT FROM WHATEVER THEY CAN FIND WHILE WE THROW HILARIOUS OBSTACLES IN THEIR WAY!
OUR JUDGES WILL AWARD THEM POINTS BASED ON TASTE AND PRESENTATION.
YOU CAN HELP YOUR FAVORITE CONTESTANT GET AHEAD BY VOTING FOR THEM TO ADD FAVORABILITY POINTS TO THEIR FINAL SCORE.
AND DON'T FORGET TO WATCH OUR WORLDWIDE BROADCAST TONIGHT FOR MORE INSIGHT ON THE ACTION WHEN WE INTERVIEW OUR CONTESTANTS!
NOW HERE'S OUR BAKERS—STRAWBERRY SHORTCAKE, THE PURPLE PIE MAN, AND LOCAL PASTRY FAVORITE, CHEF BEETALI!
RAIL DAYS

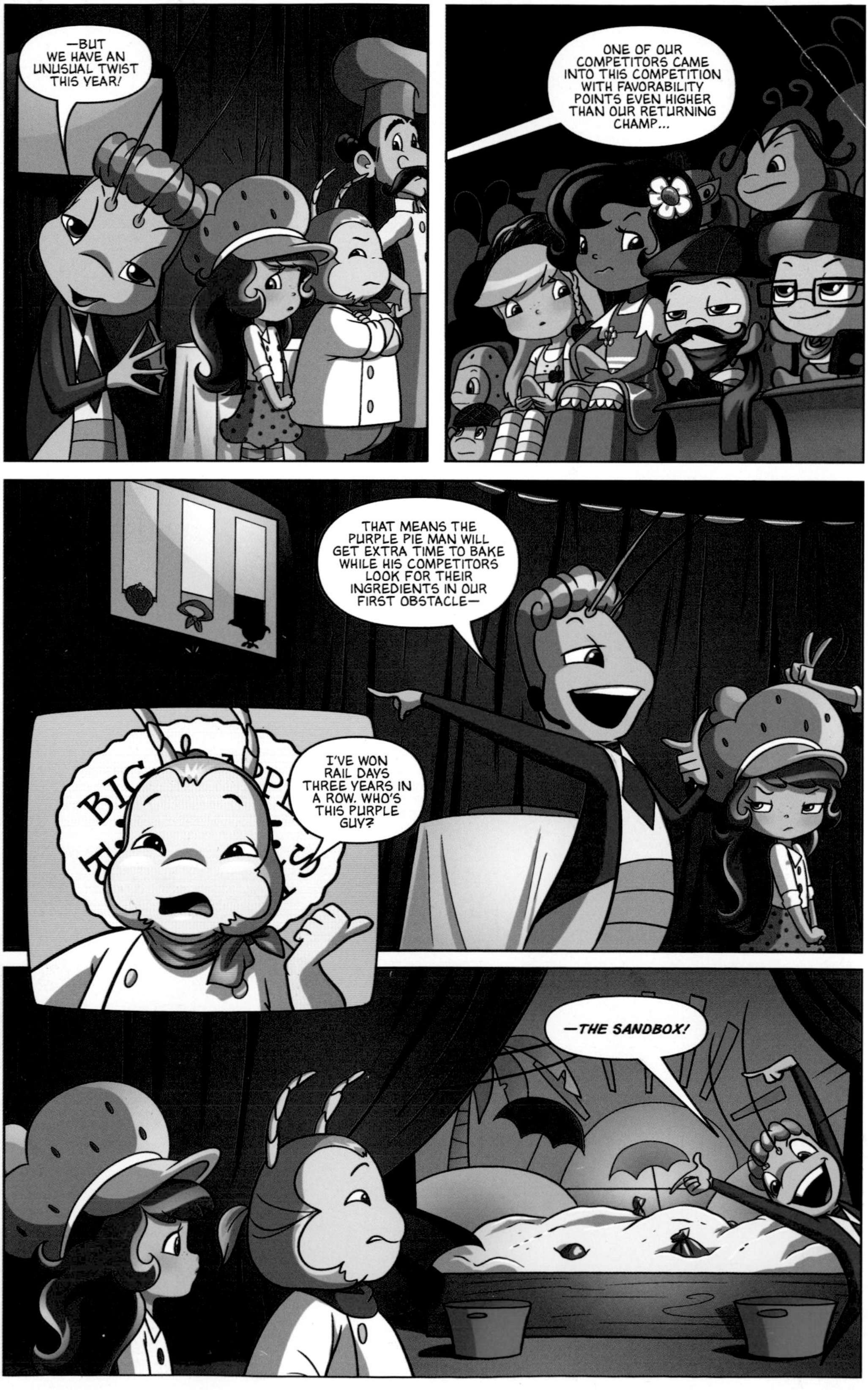
—BUT WE HAVE AN UNUSUAL TWIST THIS YEAR!
ONE OF OUR COMPETITORS CAME INTO THIS COMPETITION WITH FAVORABILITY POINTS EVEN HIGHER THAN OUR RETURNING CHAMP...
THAT MEANS THE PURPLE PIE MAN WILL GET EXTRA TIME TO BAKE WHILE HIS COMPETITORS LOOK FOR THEIR INGREDIENTS IN OUR FIRST OBSTACLE—
I'VE WON RAIL DAYS THREE YEARS IN A ROW. WHO'S THIS PURPLE GUY?
—THE SANDBOX!

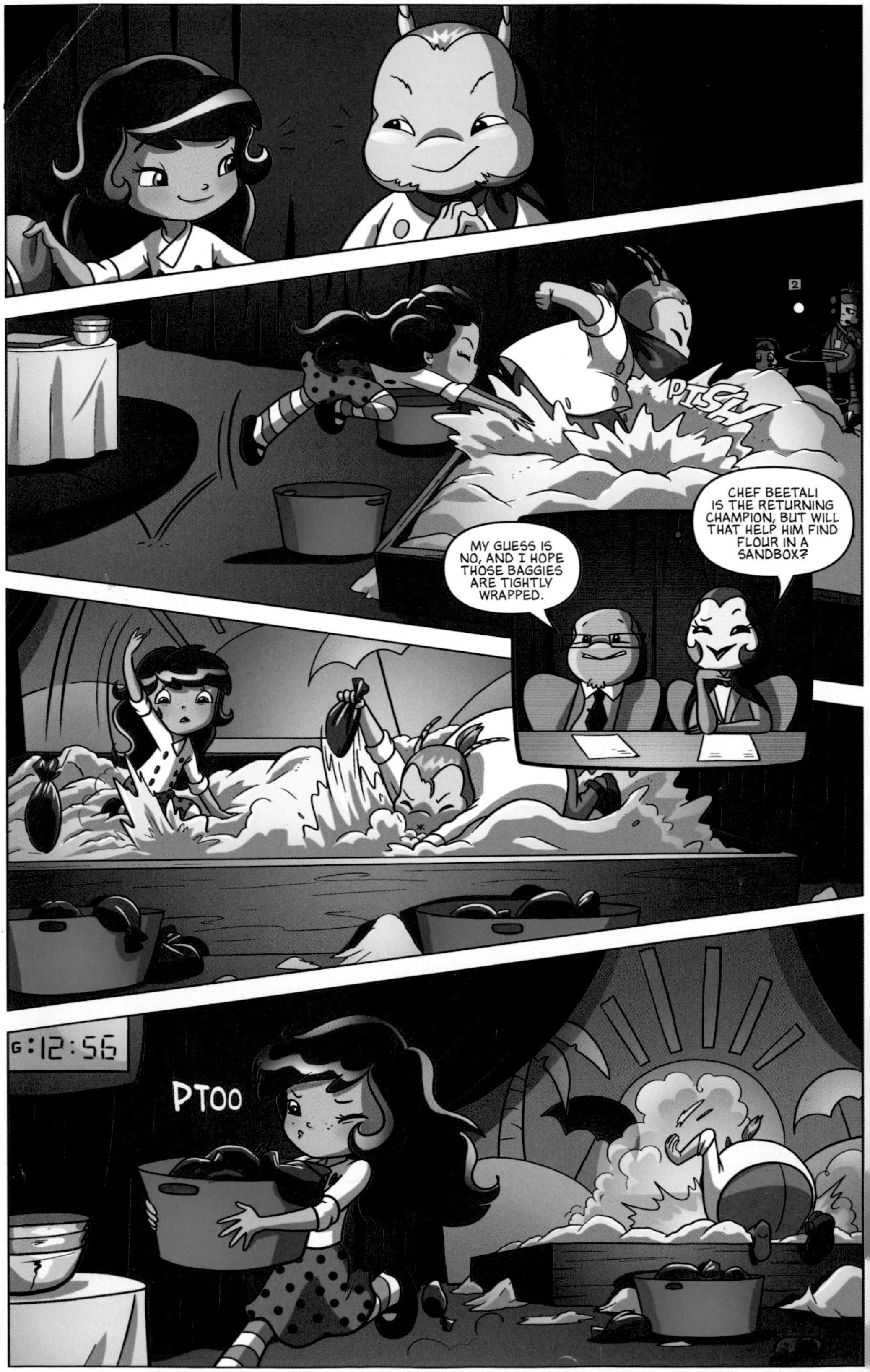
PISH
2
CHEF BEETALI IS THE RETURNING CHAMPION, BUT WILL THAT HELP HIM FIND FLOUR IN A SANDBOX?
MY GUESS IS NO, AND I HOPE THOSE BAGGIES ARE TIGHTLY WRAPPED.
G:12:56
PTOO

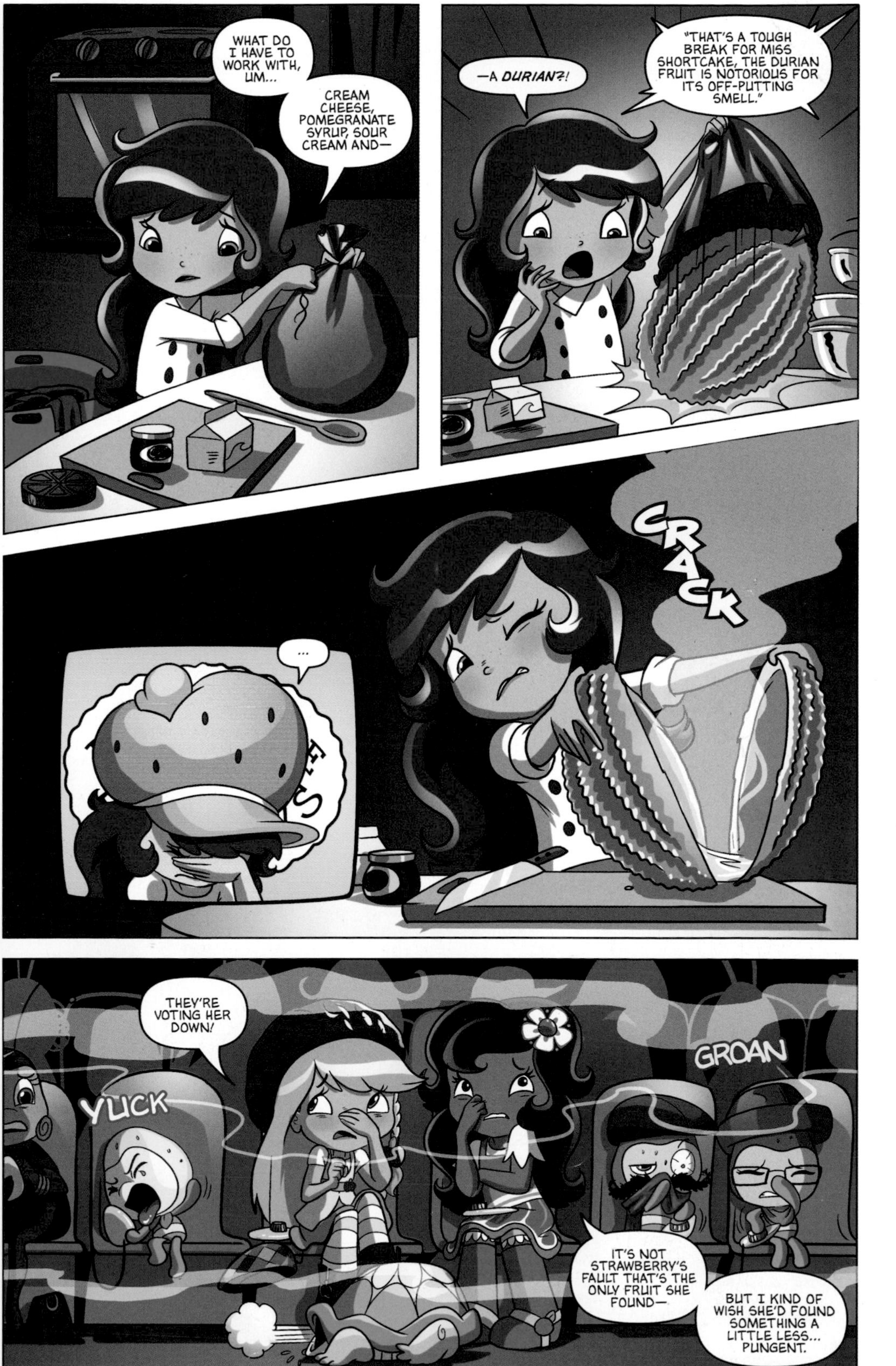
WHAT DO I HAVE TO WORK WITH, UM...
CREAM CHEESE, POMEGRANATE SYRUP, SOUR CREAM AND—
—A DURIAN?!
"THAT'S A TOUGH BREAK FOR MISS SHORTCAKE, THE DURIAN FRUIT IS NOTORIOUS FOR ITS OFF-PUTTING SMELL."
CRACK
...
THEY'RE VOTING HER DOWN!
YUCK
GROAN
IT'S NOT STRAWBERRY'S FAULT THAT'S THE ONLY FRUIT SHE FOUND—
BUT I KIND OF WISH SHE'D FOUND SOMETHING A LITTLE LESS... PUNGENT.

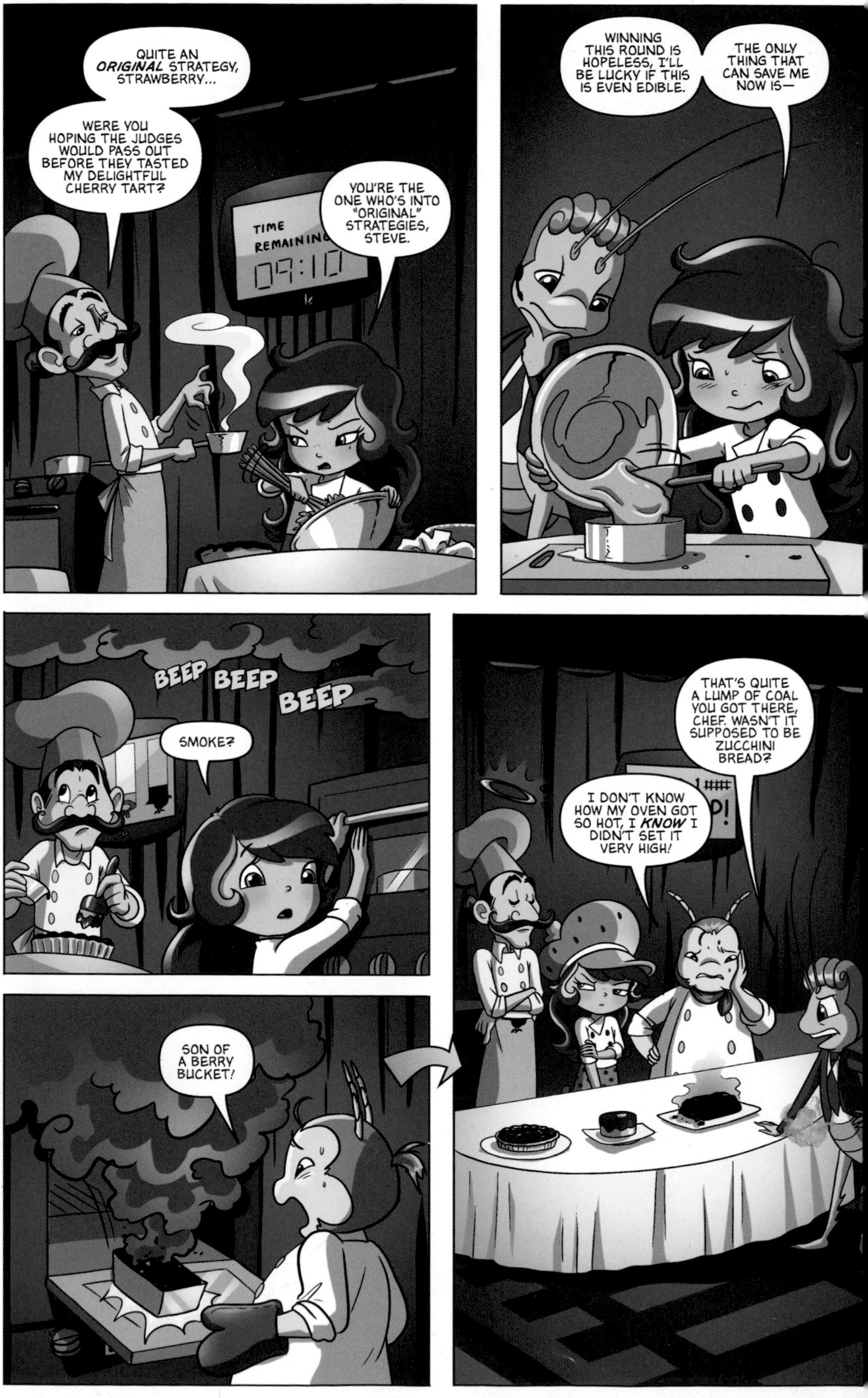
QUITE AN ORIGINAL STRATEGY, STRAWBERRY...
WERE YOU HOPING THE JUDGES WOULD PASS OUT BEFORE THEY TASTED MY DELIGHTFUL CHERRY TART?
TIME REMAINING
09:10
YOU'RE THE ONE WHO'S INTO "ORIGINAL" STRATEGIES, STEVE.
WINNING THIS ROUND IS HOPELESS, I'LL BE LUCKY IF THIS IS EVEN EDIBLE.
THE ONLY THING THAT CAN SAVE ME NOW IS—
BEEP BEEP BEEP
SMOKE?
SON OF A BERRY BUCKET!
THAT'S QUITE A LUMP OF COAL YOU GOT THERE, CHEF. WASN'T IT SUPPOSED TO BE ZUCCHINI BREAD?
I DON'T KNOW HOW MY OVEN GOT SO HOT, I KNOW I DIDN'T SET IT VERY HIGH!

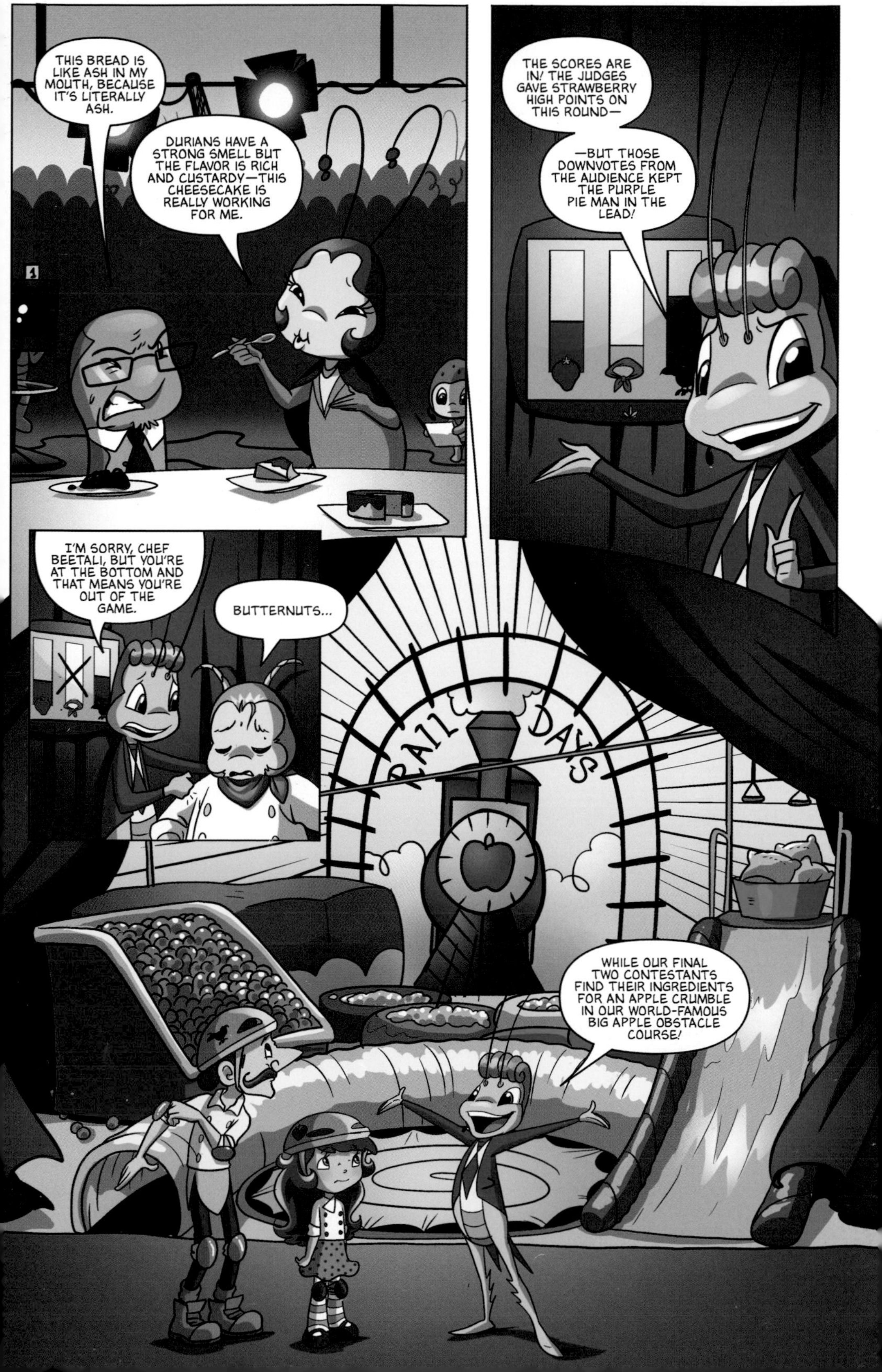
THIS BREAD IS LIKE ASH IN MY MOUTH, BECAUSE IT'S LITERALLY ASH.
DURIANS HAVE A STRONG SMELL BUT THE FLAVOR IS RICH AND CUSTARDY—THIS CHEESECAKE IS REALLY WORKING FOR ME.
THE SCORES ARE IN! THE JUDGES GAVE STRAWBERRY HIGH POINTS ON THIS ROUND—
—BUT THOSE DOWNVOTES FROM THE AUDIENCE KEPT THE PURPLE PIE MAN IN THE LEAD!
I'M SORRY, CHEF BEETALI, BUT YOU'RE AT THE BOTTOM AND THAT MEANS YOU'RE OUT OF THE GAME.
BUTTERNUTS...
RAIL DAYS
WHILE OUR FINAL TWO CONTESTANTS FIND THEIR INGREDIENTS FOR AN APPLE CRUMBLE IN OUR WORLD-FAMOUS BIG APPLE OBSTACLE COURSE!

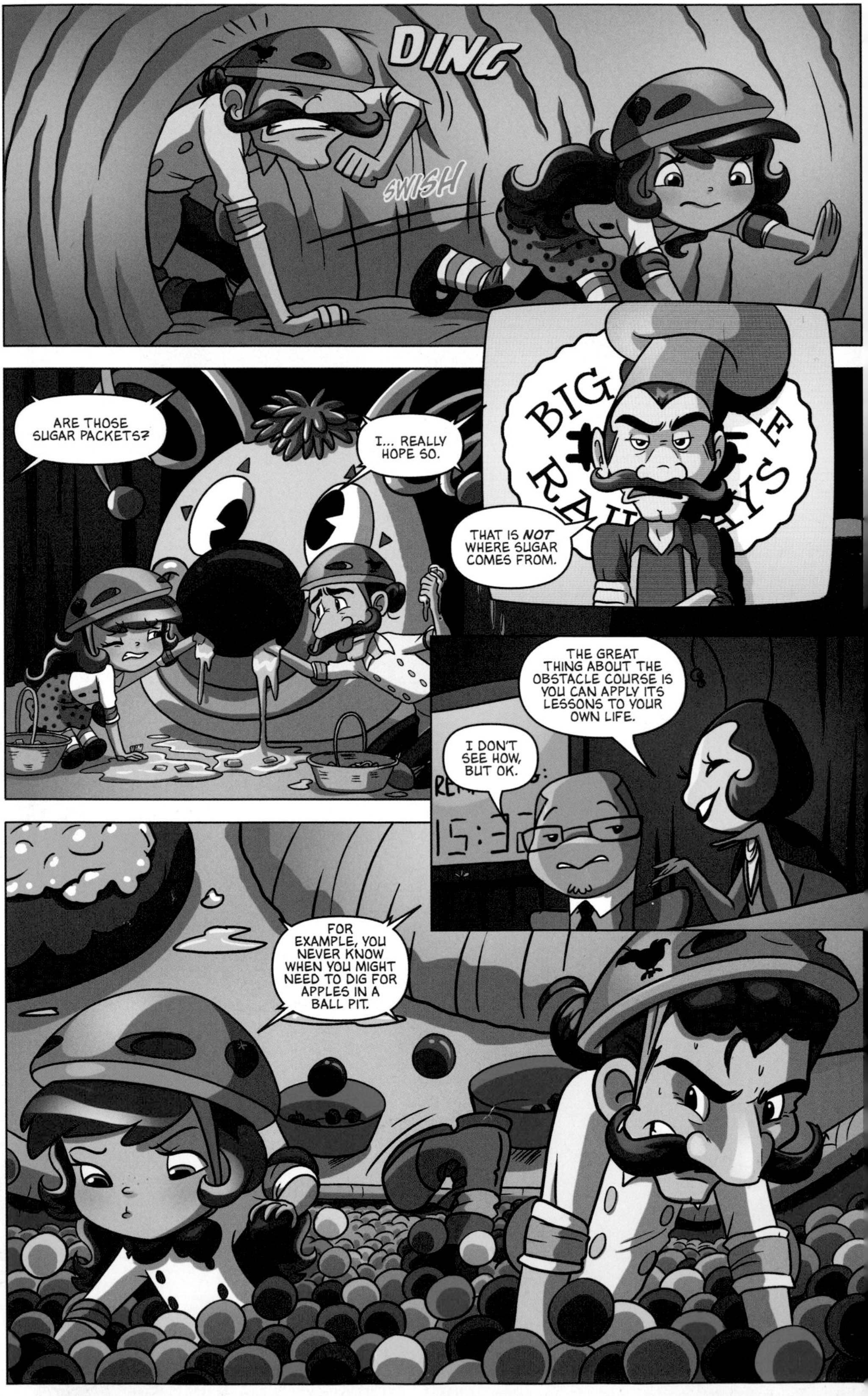
DING
SWISH
ARE THOSE SUGAR PACKETS?
I... REALLY HOPE SO.
THAT IS NOT WHERE SUGAR COMES FROM.
THE GREAT THING ABOUT THE OBSTACLE COURSE IS YOU CAN APPLY ITS LESSONS TO YOUR OWN LIFE.
I DON'T SEE HOW, BUT OK.
FOR EXAMPLE, YOU NEVER KNOW WHEN YOU MIGHT NEED TO DIG FOR APPLES IN A BALL PIT.

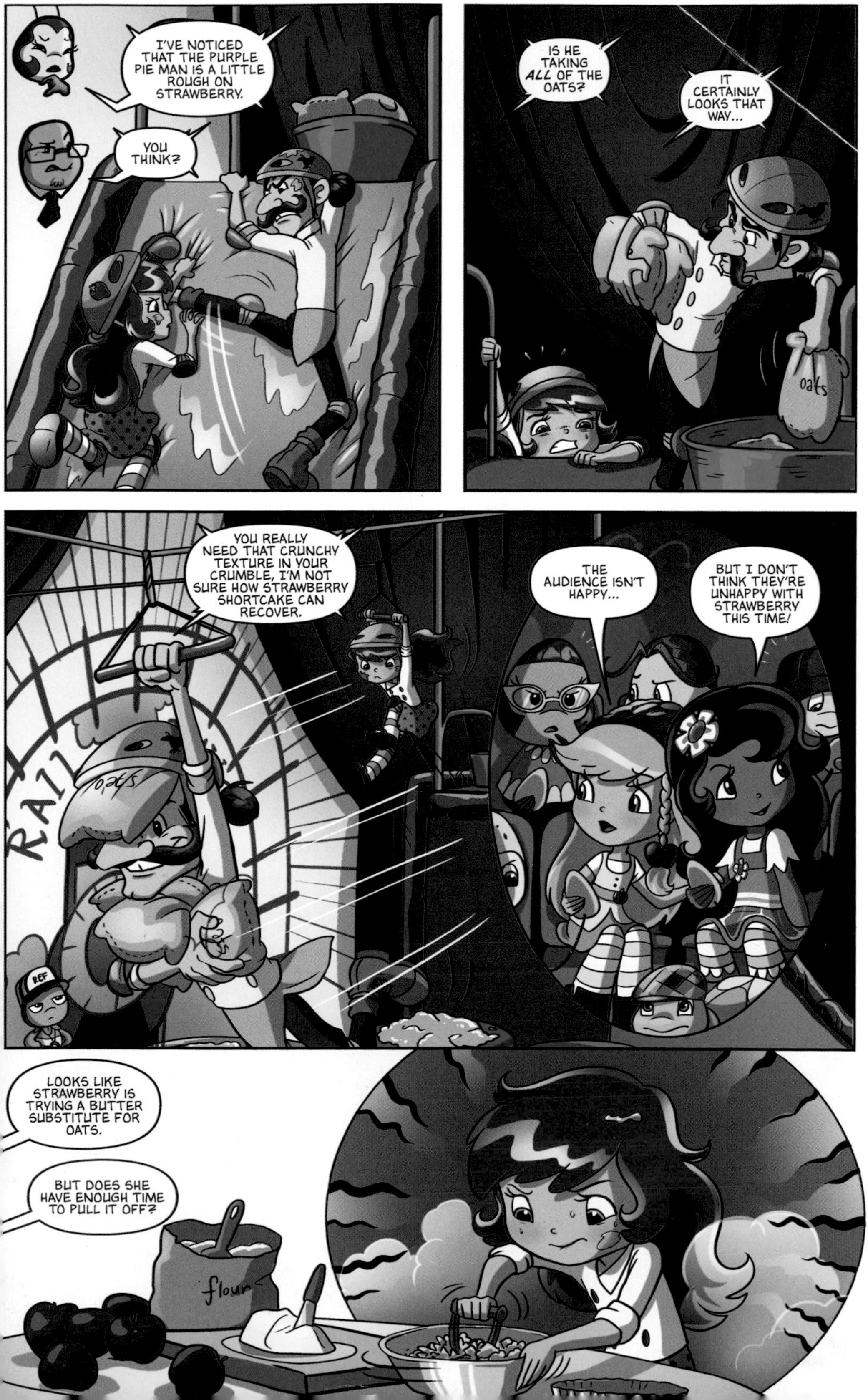

I'VE NOTICED THAT THE PURPLE PIE MAN IS A LITTLE ROUGH ON STRAWBERRY.
YOU THINK?
IS HE TAKING *ALL* OF THE OATS?
IT CERTAINLY LOOKS THAT WAY...
oats
YOU REALLY NEED THAT CRUNCHY TEXTURE IN YOUR CRUMBLE, I'M NOT SURE HOW STRAWBERRY SHORTCAKE CAN RECOVER.
THE AUDIENCE ISN'T HAPPY...
BUT I DON'T THINK THEY'RE UNHAPPY WITH STRAWBERRY THIS TIME!
oats
REF
LOOKS LIKE STRAWBERRY IS TRYING A BUTTER SUBSTITUTE FOR OATS.
BUT DOES SHE HAVE ENOUGH TIME TO PULL IT OFF?
flour

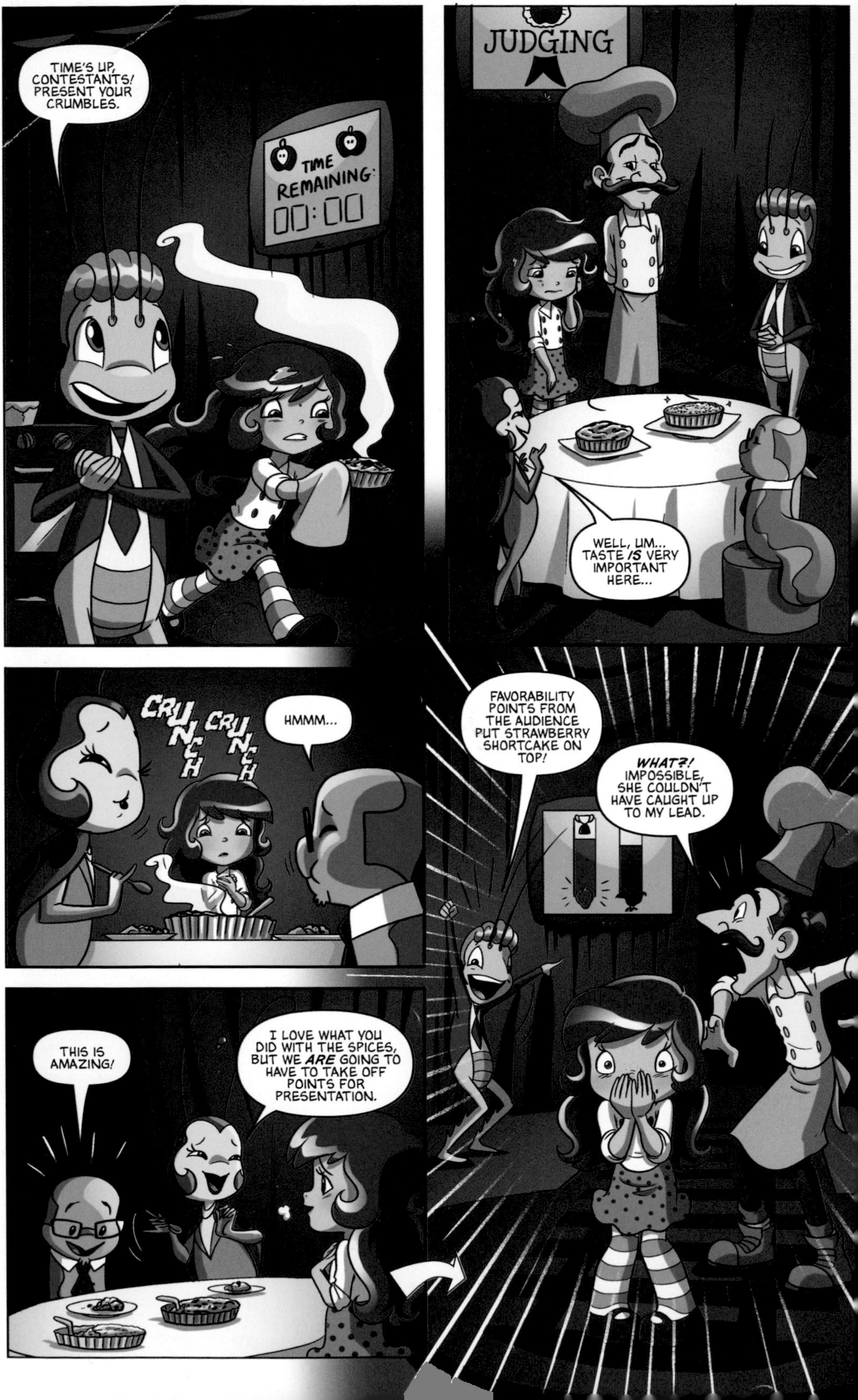
TIME'S UP, CONTESTANTS! PRESENT YOUR CRUMBLES.
TIME REMAINING:
00:00
JUDGING
WELL, UM... TASTE IS VERY IMPORTANT HERE...
CRUNCH CRUNCH
HMMM...
THIS IS AMAZING!
I LOVE WHAT YOU DID WITH THE SPICES, BUT WE ARE GOING TO HAVE TO TAKE OFF POINTS FOR PRESENTATION.
FAVORABILITY POINTS FROM THE AUDIENCE PUT STRAWBERRY SHORTCAKE ON TOP!
WHAT?! IMPOSSIBLE, SHE COULDN'T HAVE CAUGHT UP TO MY LEAD.

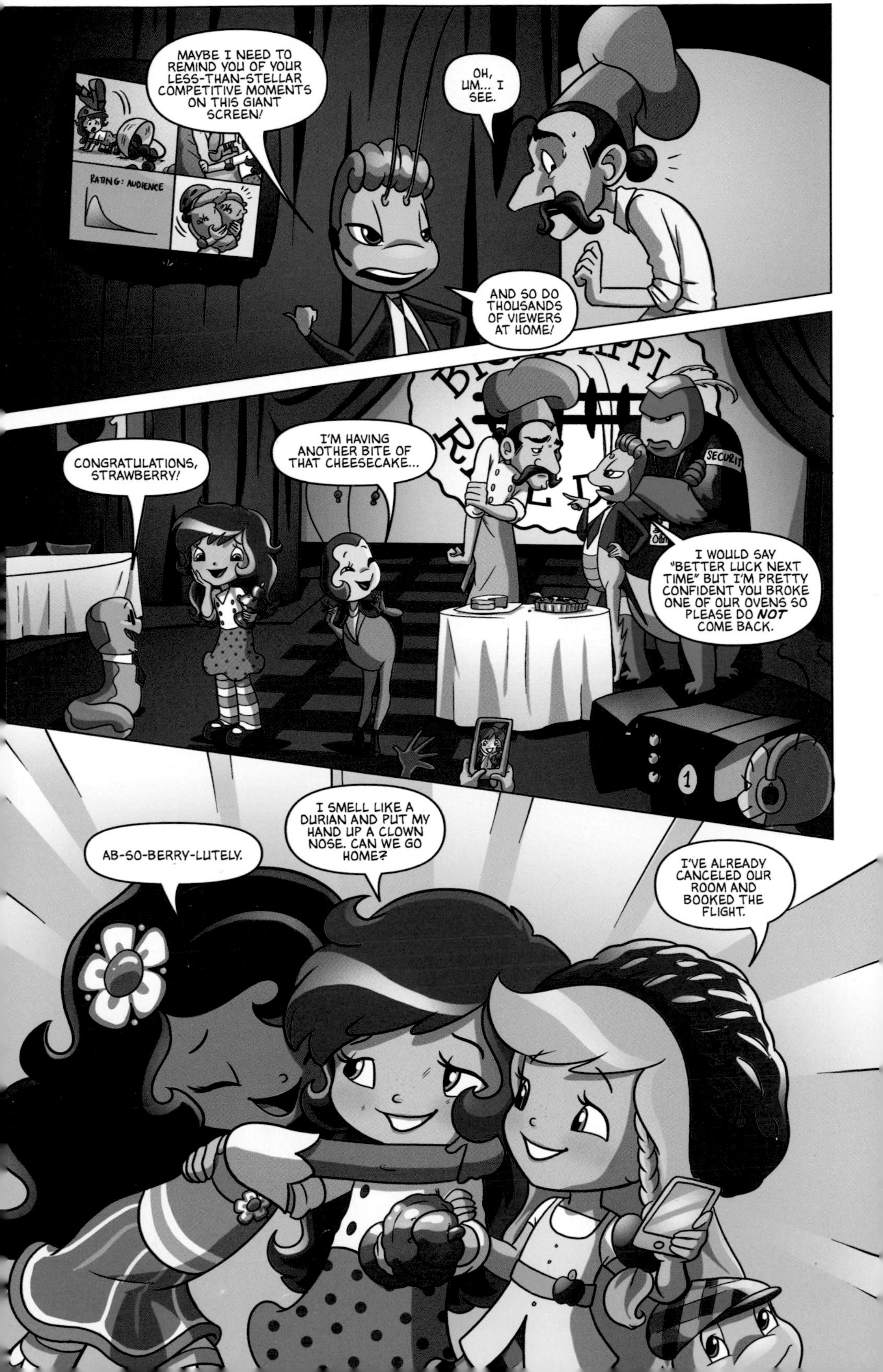
MAYBE I NEED TO REMIND YOU OF YOUR LESS-THAN-STELLAR COMPETITIVE MOMENTS ON THIS GIANT SCREEN!
RATING: AUDIENCE
OH, UM... I SEE.
AND SO DO THOUSANDS OF VIEWERS AT HOME!
CONGRATULATIONS, STRAWBERRY!
I'M HAVING ANOTHER BITE OF THAT CHEESECAKE...
I WOULD SAY "BETTER LUCK NEXT TIME" BUT I'M PRETTY CONFIDENT YOU BROKE ONE OF OUR OVENS SO PLEASE DO NOT COME BACK.
AB-SO-BERRY-LUTELY.
I SMELL LIKE A DURIAN AND PUT MY HAND UP A CLOWN NOSE. CAN WE GO HOME?
I'VE ALREADY CANCELED OUR ROOM AND BOOKED THE FLIGHT.

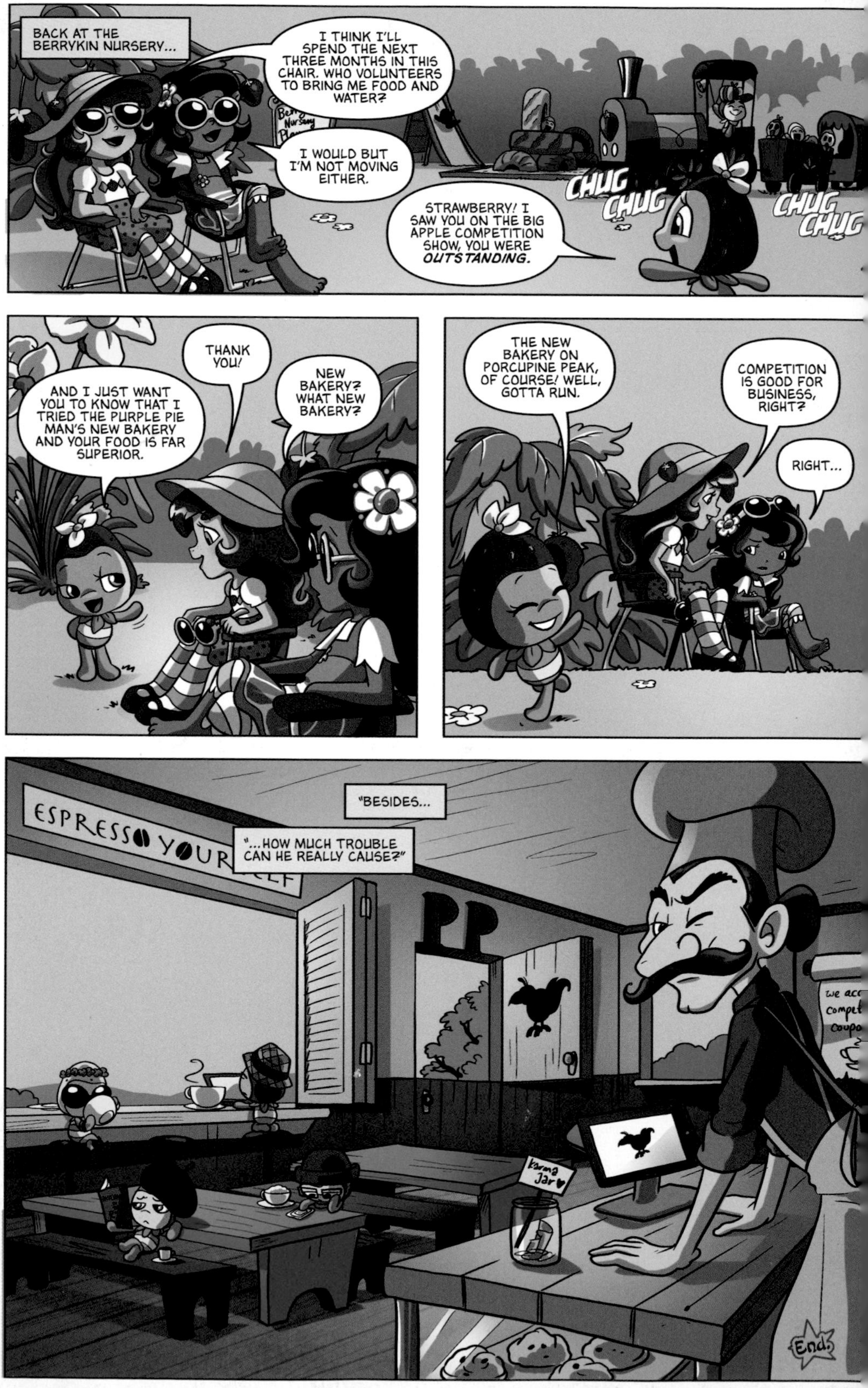
BACK AT THE BERRYKIN NURSERY...
I THINK I'LL SPEND THE NEXT THREE MONTHS IN THIS CHAIR. WHO VOLUNTEERS TO BRING ME FOOD AND WATER?
I WOULD BUT I'M NOT MOVING EITHER.
CHUG CHUG
CHUG CHUG
STRAWBERRY! I SAW YOU ON THE BIG APPLE COMPETITION SHOW, YOU WERE OUTSTANDING.
THANK YOU!
AND I JUST WANT YOU TO KNOW THAT I TRIED THE PURPLE PIE MAN'S NEW BAKERY AND YOUR FOOD IS FAR SUPERIOR.
NEW BAKERY? WHAT NEW BAKERY?
THE NEW BAKERY ON PORCUPINE PEAK, OF COURSE! WELL, GOTTA RUN.
COMPETITION IS GOOD FOR BUSINESS, RIGHT?
RIGHT...
"BESIDES...
"...HOW MUCH TROUBLE CAN HE REALLY CAUSE?"
ESPRESSO YOUR
PP
Karma Jar
End.

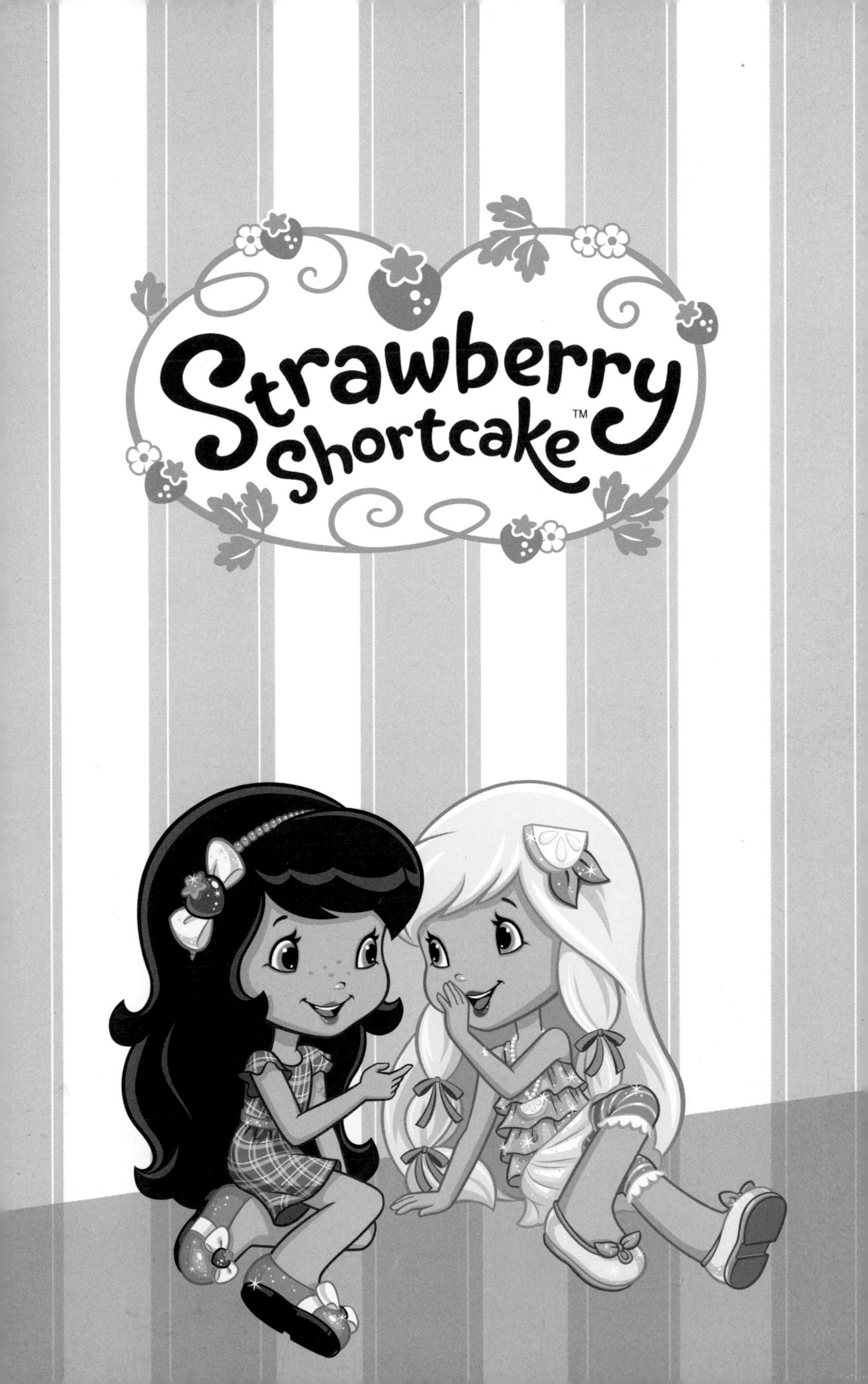
Strawberry Shortcake™

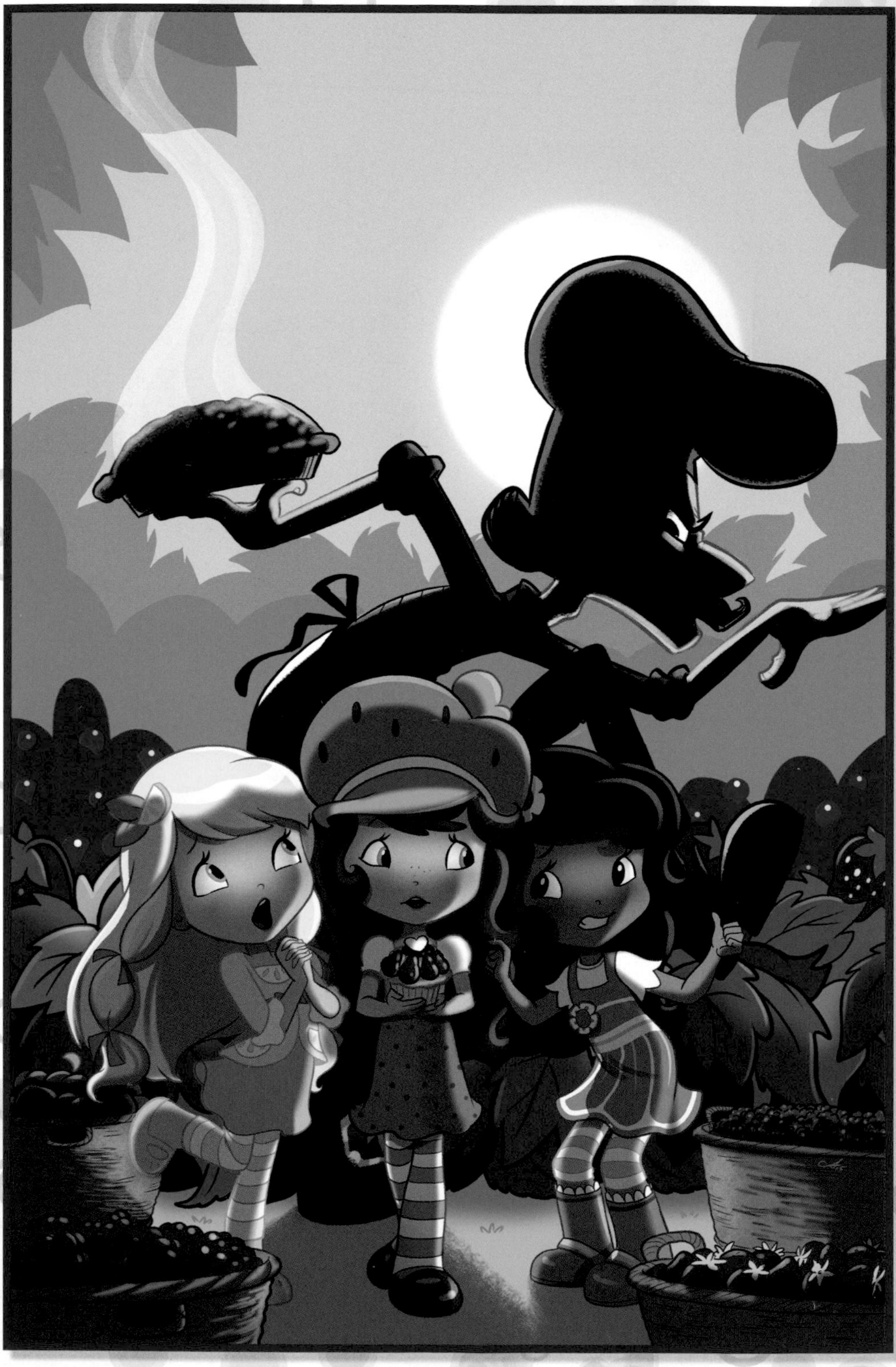

COVER ART BY
Amy Mebberson

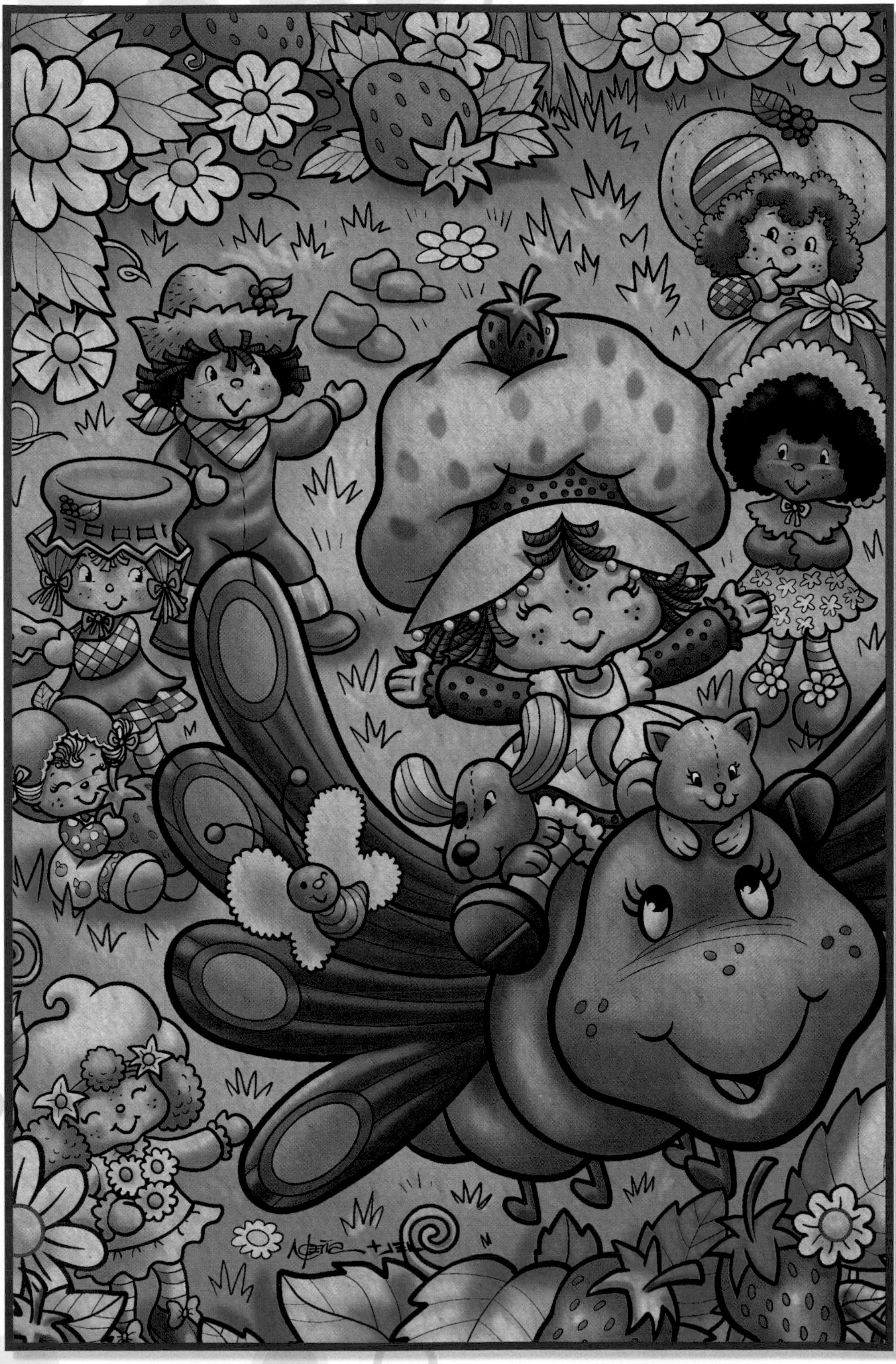

COVER ART BY
Nico Peña

COLORS BY
Jordi Escuin

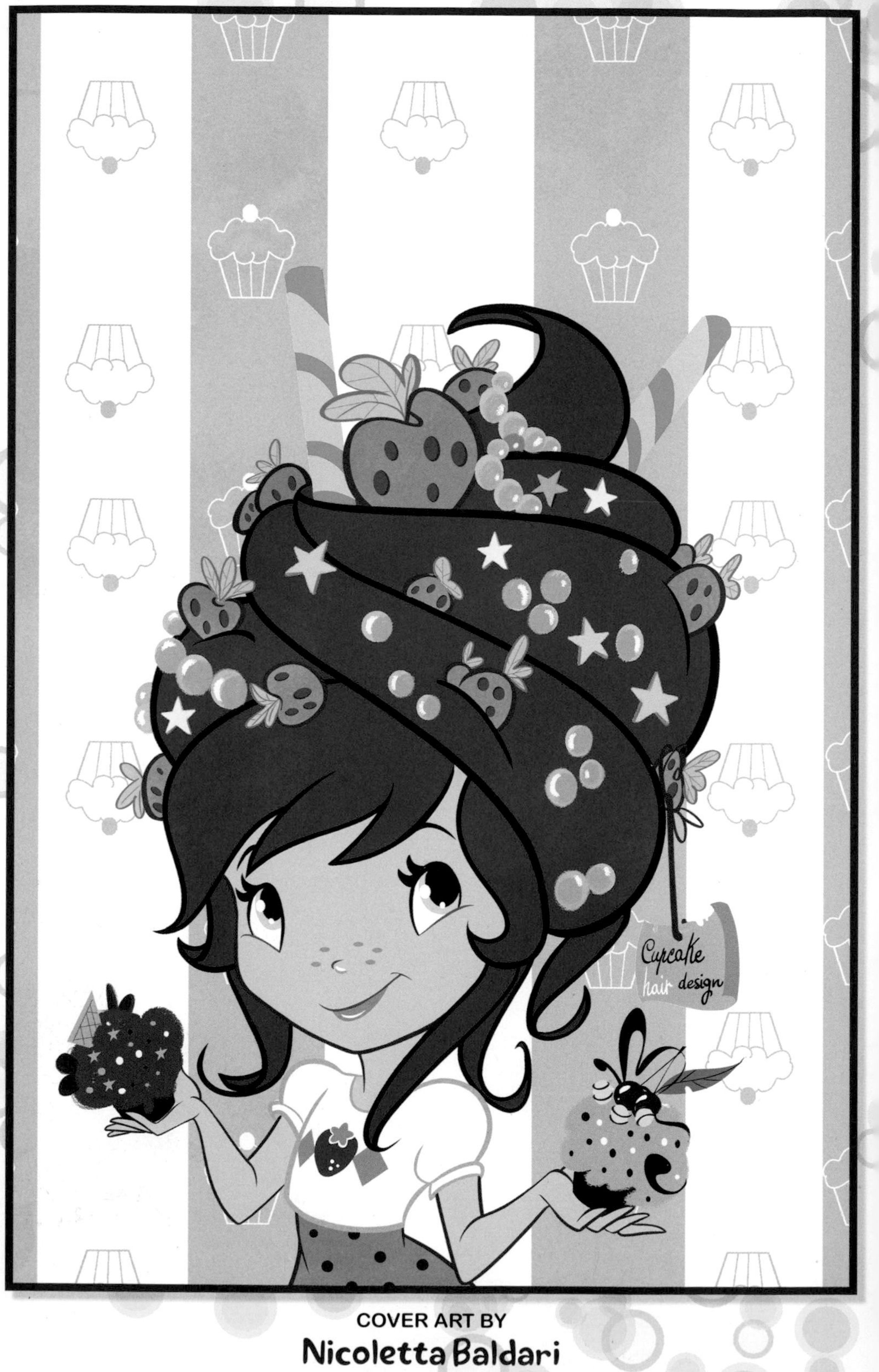
Cupcake hair design

COVER ART BY
Nicoletta Baldari

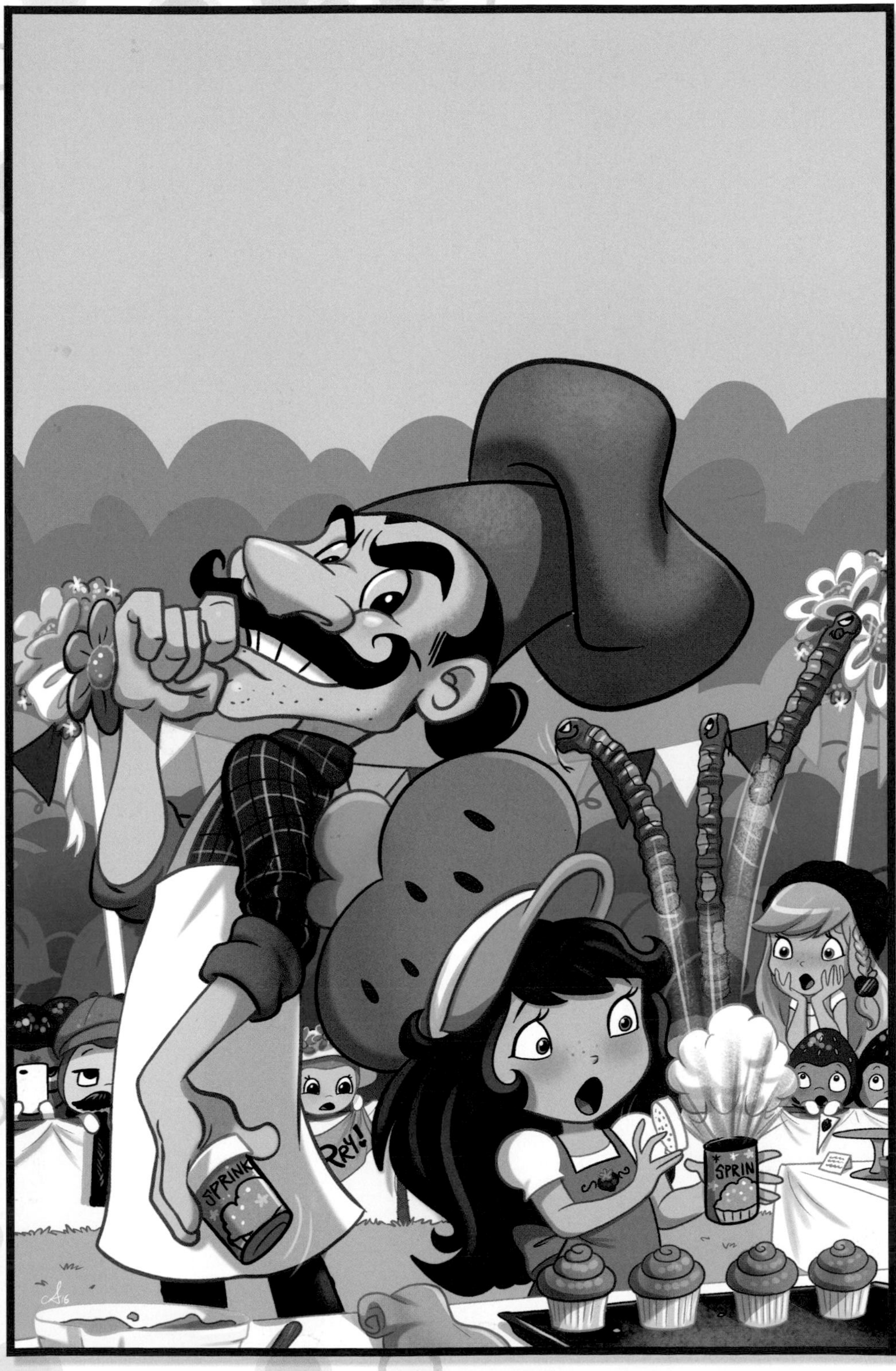
RRY!
SPRINK
SPRIN

COVER ART BY
Amy Mebberson

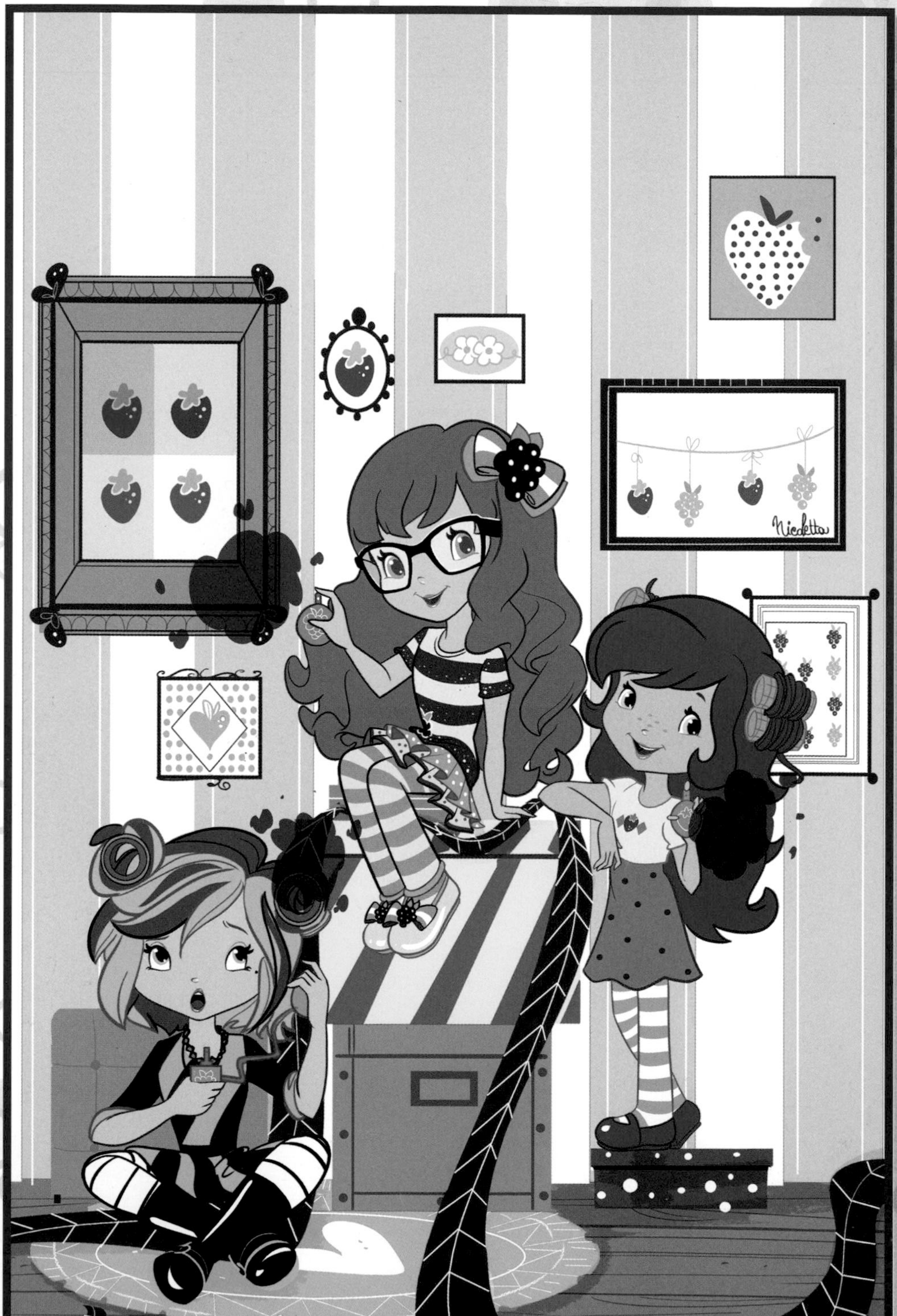
Nicoletta

COVER ART BY
Nicoletta Baldari

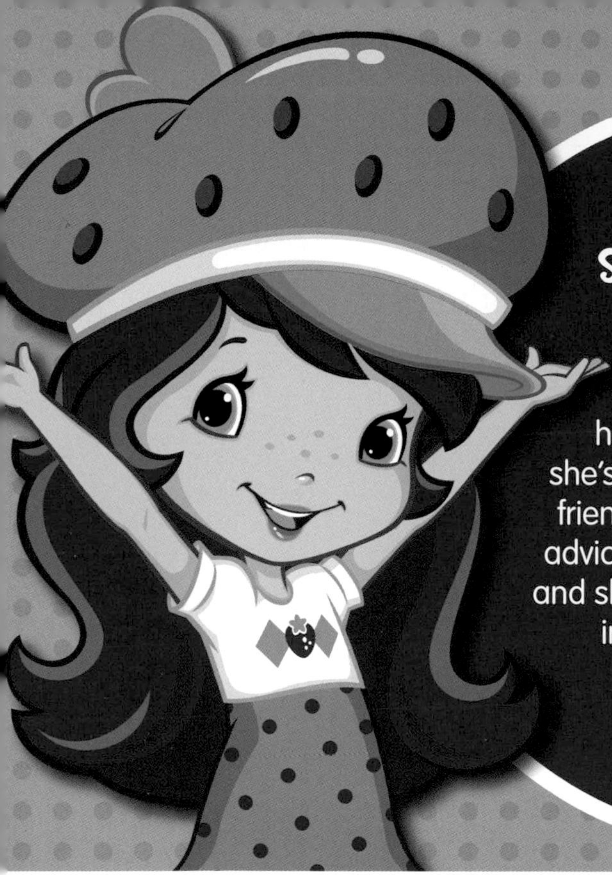

Strawberry Shortcake

She is everybody's berry best friend. When she's not running her Berry Café in Berry Bitty City, she's hosting get-togethers with her friends or offering them help and advice. Her optimism is contagious and she always sees big possiblilities in everything–and everyone! With Strawberry Shortcake on your side... Anything is possible!

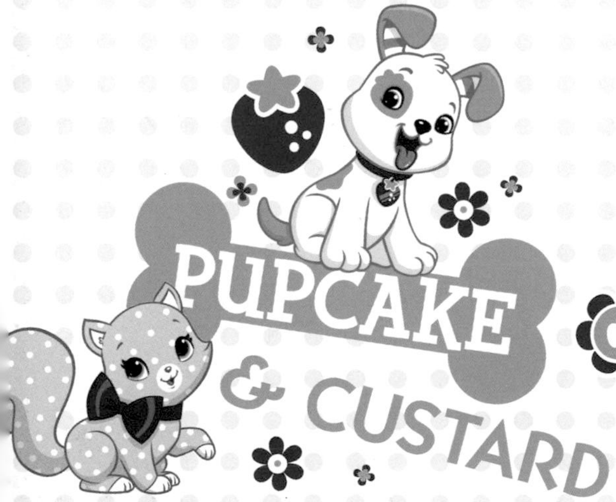

PUPCAKE & CUSTARD

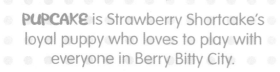

PUPCAKE is Strawberry Shortcake's loyal puppy who loves to play with everyone in Berry Bitty City.

CUSTARD is Strawberry Shortcake's purr-fect pet kitty. She's cuddly, sweet, and absolutely adorable!

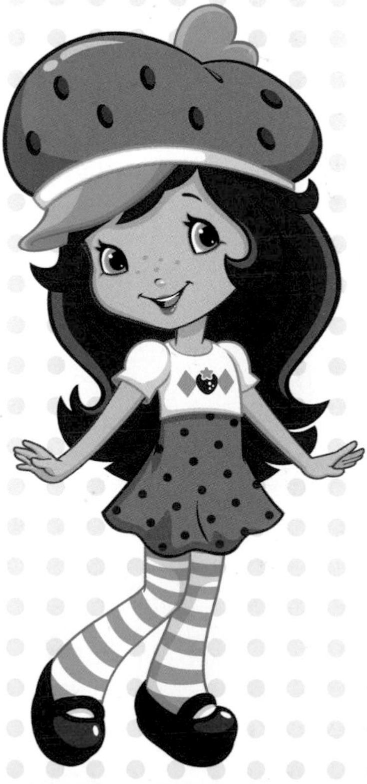

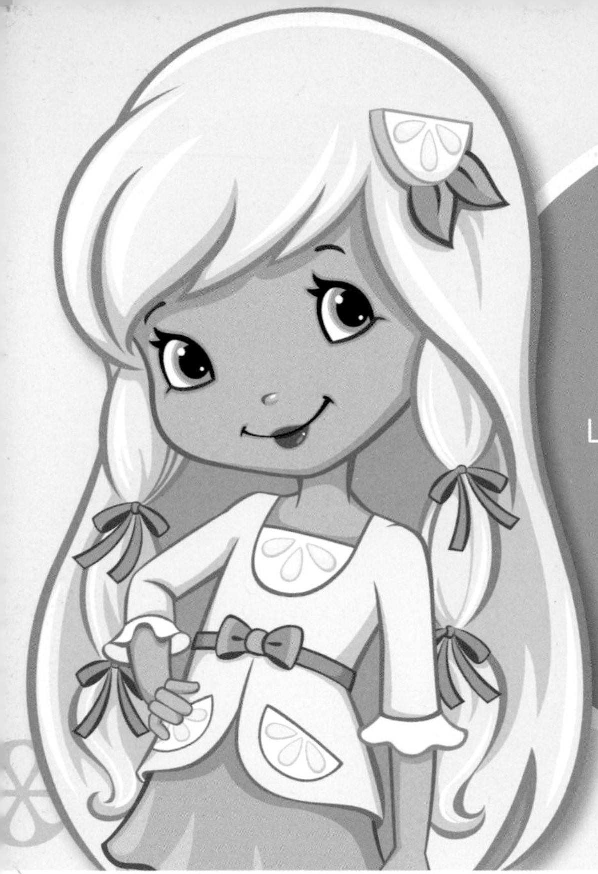

Lemon Meringue

She is an expert with a comb and blow-dryer. She runs the Lemon Salon where all the girls get their hair styled. Lemon is very fun to be around and loves to keep everyone up to date on what's happening in Berry Bitty City.

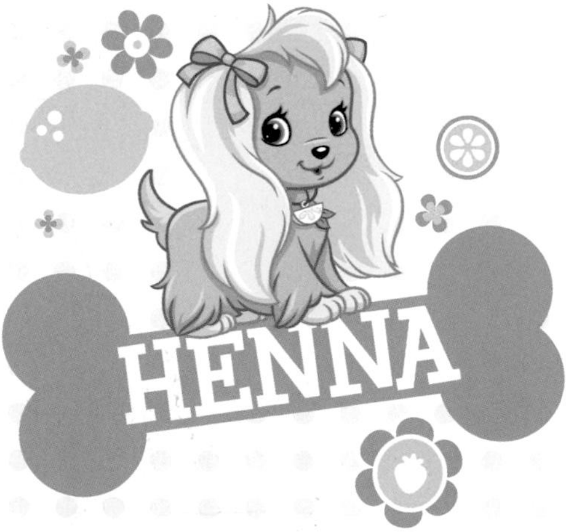
HENNA

Lemon's spaniel puppy, who loves getting her long hair styled in Lemon's salon.

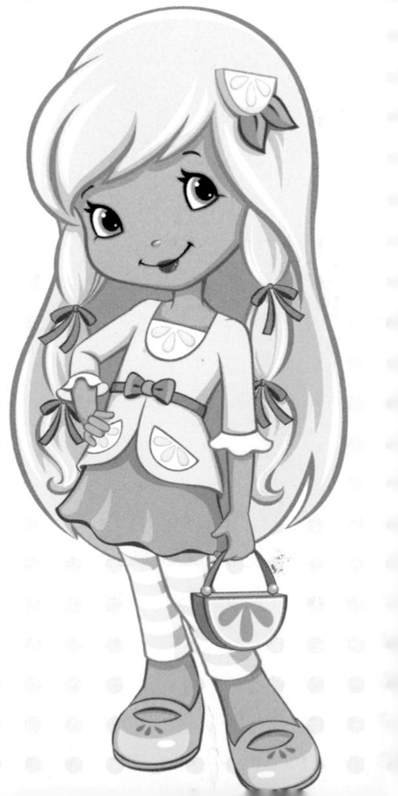

Cherry Jam

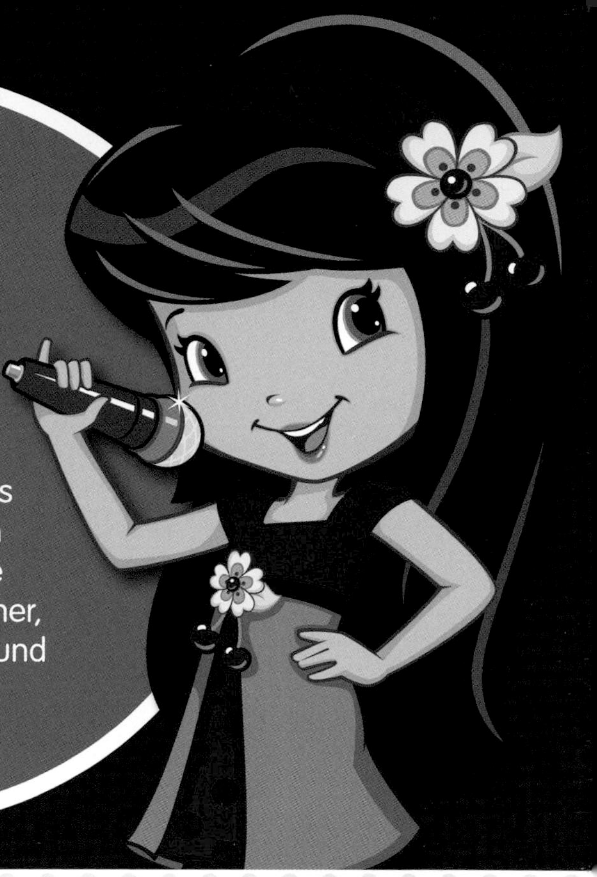

She is Berry Bitty City's most famous resident pop star! When the singing superstar is offstage, her cheery charm helps her fit right in as the town's favorite music teacher, voice coach, and all-around fabulous friend!

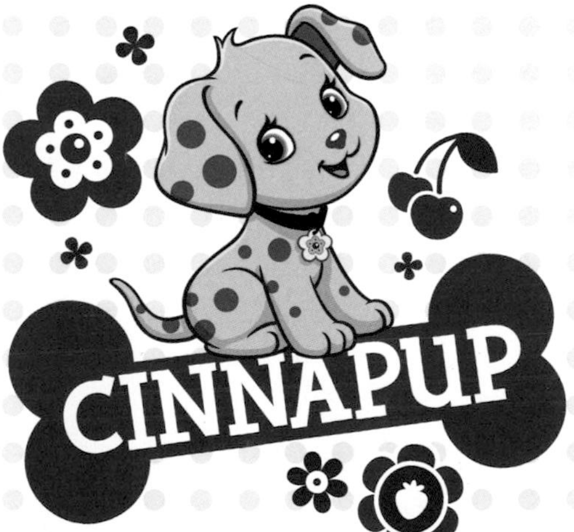
CINNAPUP

She is Cherry Jam's Dalmation. She loves to howl and bark along with Cherry as she sings. They are quite the entertaining pair!

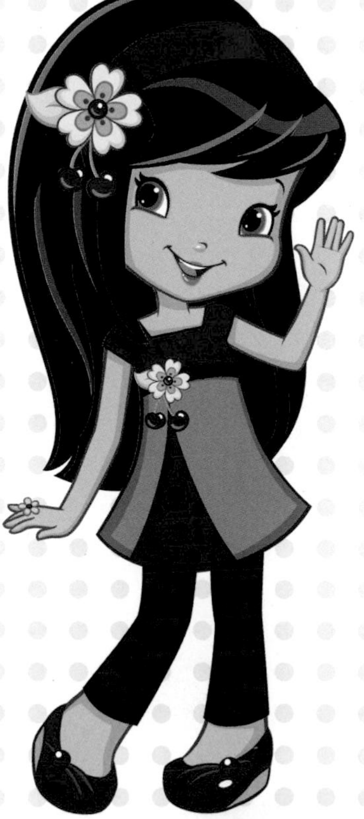

Orange Blossom

She is Berry energetic and is all about solving problems with a smile. She runs Orange Mart, a little store that holds everything you could ever need. Orange loves being helpful and always puts everyone in a good mood.

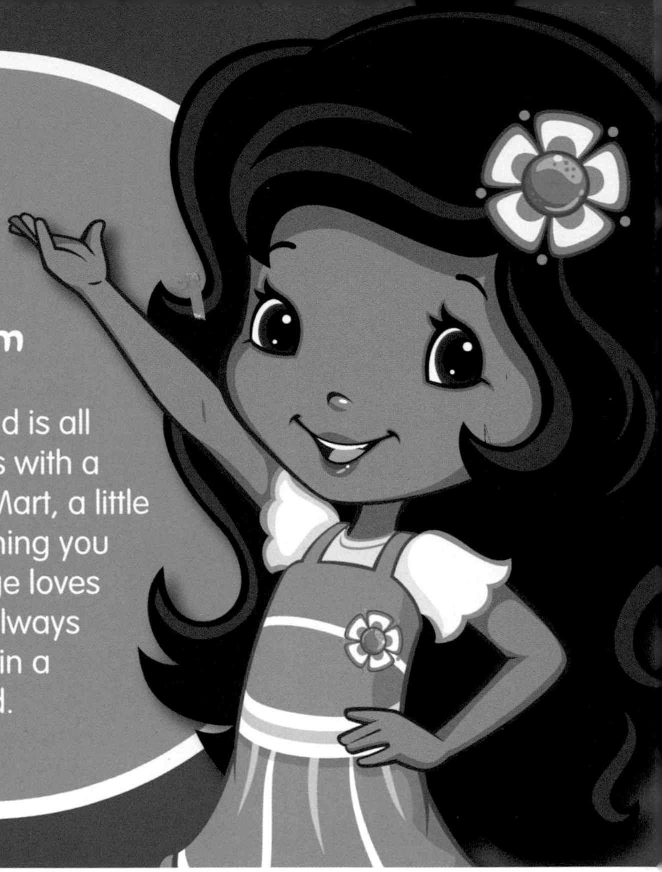

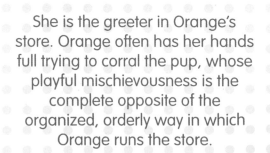

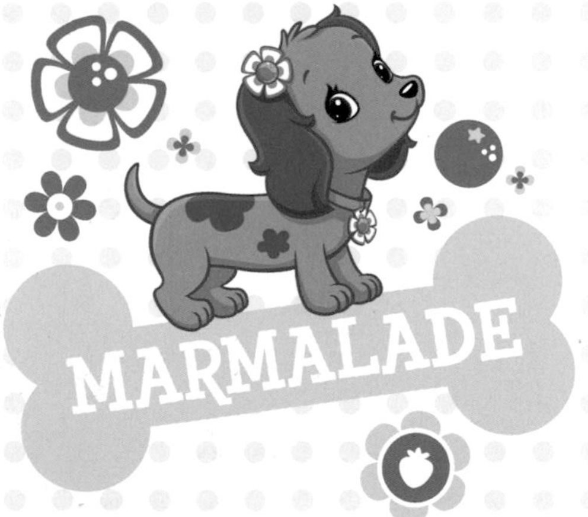
MARMALADE

She is the greeter in Orange's store. Orange often has her hands full trying to corral the pup, whose playful mischievousness is the complete opposite of the organized, orderly way in which Orange runs the store.

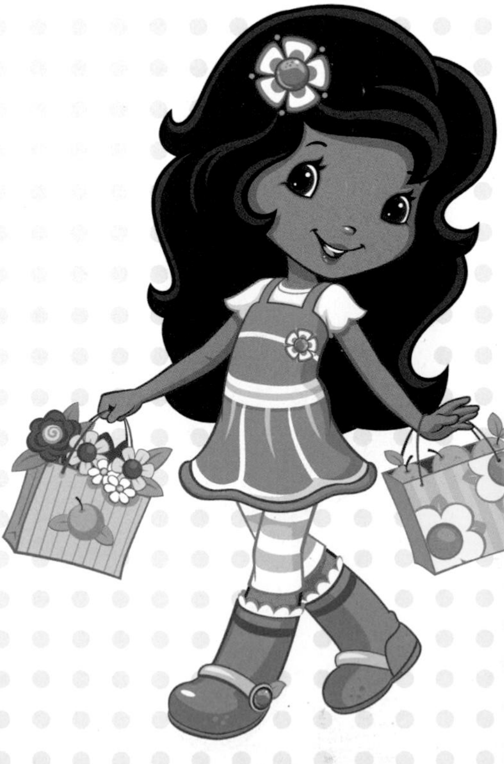

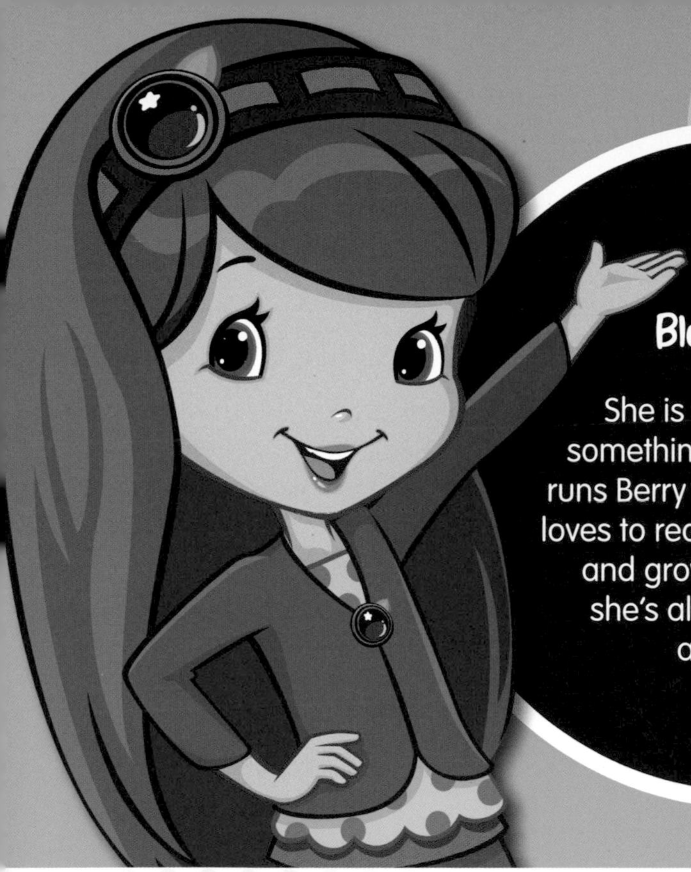

Blueberry Muffin

She is super smart and knows something about everything. She runs Berry Bitty City's bookstore and loves to read about how things work and grow. Her best buds know she's always there for them—a true-blue friend to the end.

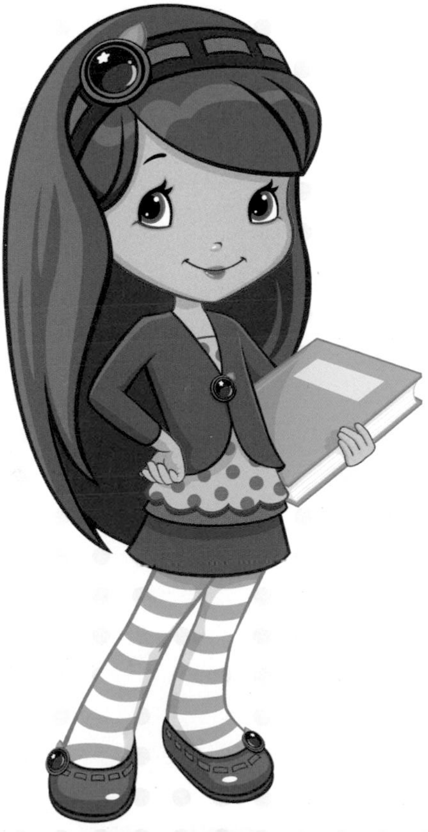

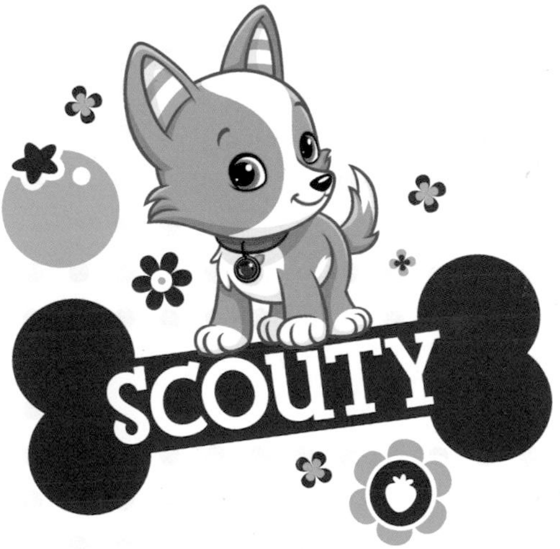
SCOUTY

He is an especially smart collie with a particularly good nose for tracking and finding things—a talent that endears him to his owner, mystery novel lover, Blueberry.

Plum Pudding

She is always on the move and seems to hear a happy dance beat wherever she goes. She's a great dancer who teaches all styles of dance at her Sweet Beats Studio. Plum's kind heart and quirky ways make her a favorite friend in Berry Bitty City.

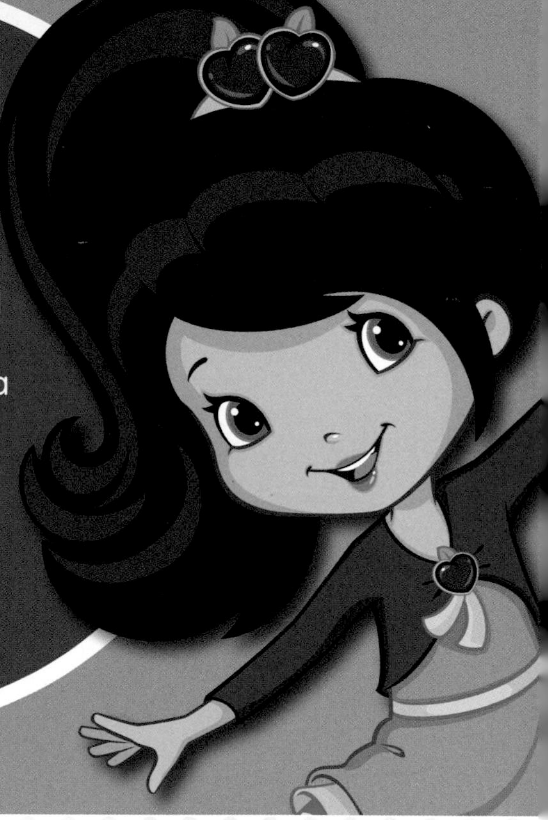

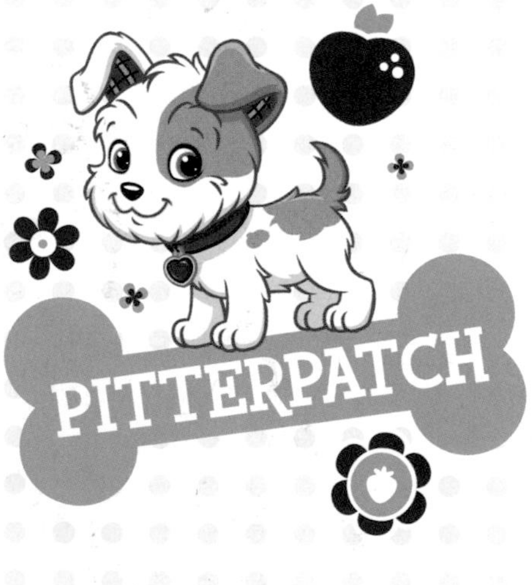
PITTERPATCH

He is a perfect match for Plum. This terrier's exuberant energy is a great complement to Plum's dancing.

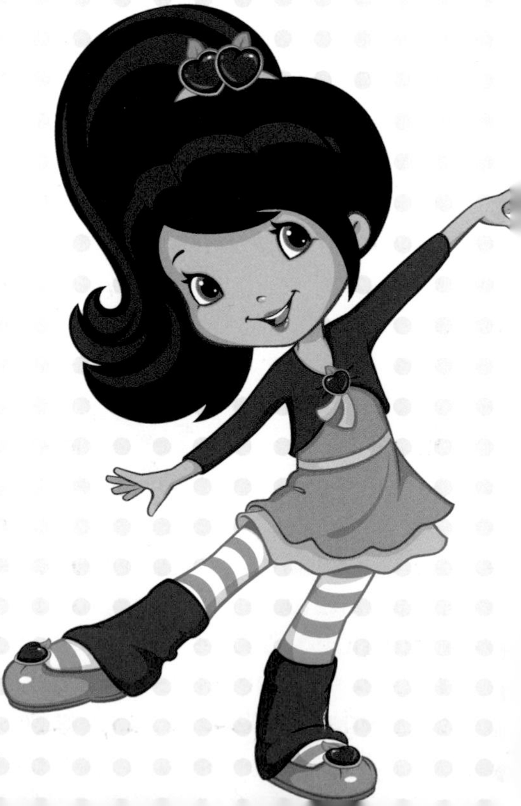

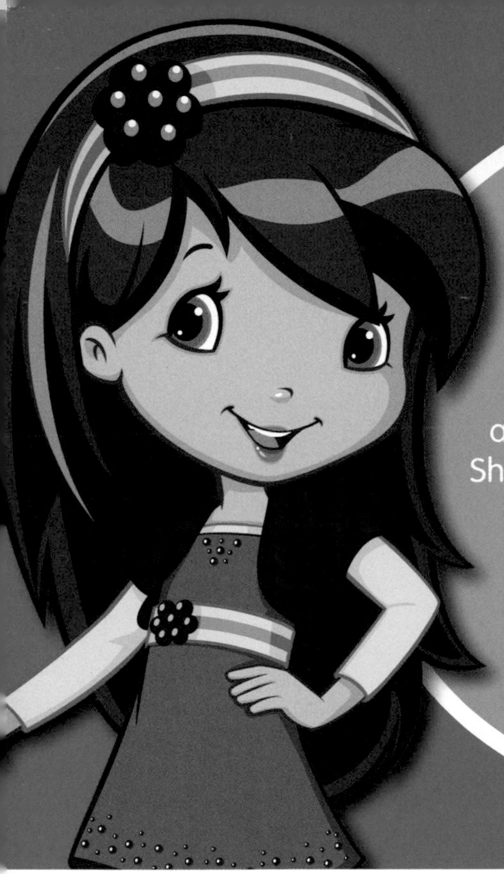

Raspberry Torte

Super-stylish, she loves giving fashion advice to all the girls in Berry Bitty City. She even owns and runs Fresh Fashions, a very trendy boutique.

Raspberry's friends know they can always count on her for the berry latest styles– and true friendship, too!

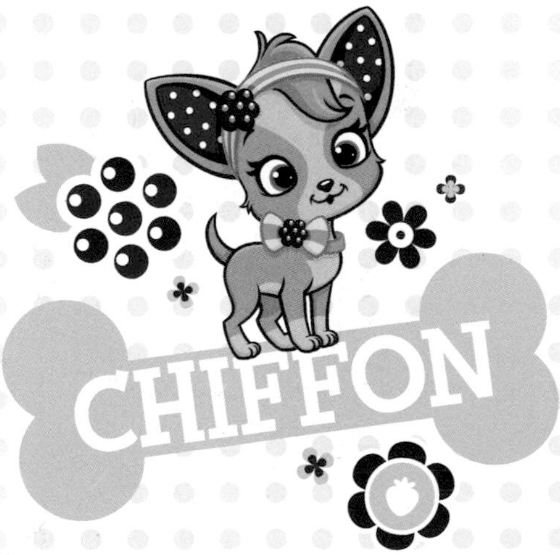
CHIFFON

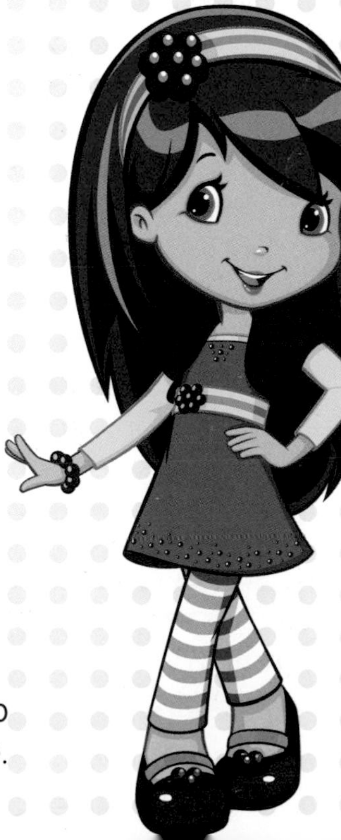

She is fashion-designer Raspberry's Chihuahua. In addition to modeling Raspberry's latest dog fashions, her miniature size makes her a perfect fit to be carried around in Raspberry's purse.

Sweet Grapes & Sour Grapes

Although they are twin sisters, they couldn't be more different!

Sweet is the nicest person ever, with her lighthearted, friendly personality. Sour likes to spice things up with her realistic and zesty attitude! Together the sisters run a food truck. They're both fun and funny in their own special ways, which makes hanging out with them such a good time!

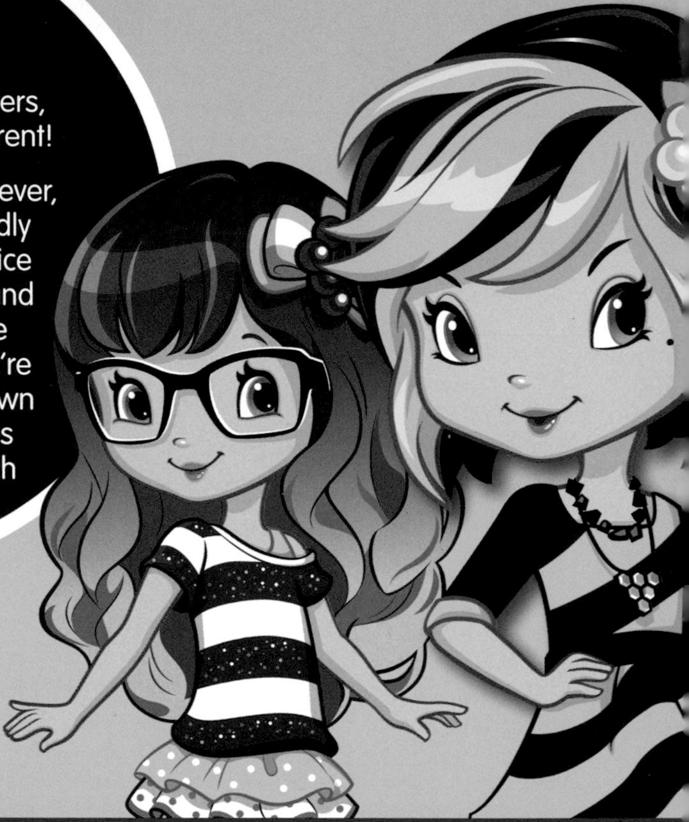

Apple Dumplin'

She is Strawberry's cousin who just moved to Berry Bitty City. She's a world traveler and resident blogger. She just loves adventure, and she always has an exciting story to share from all the places she's visited!

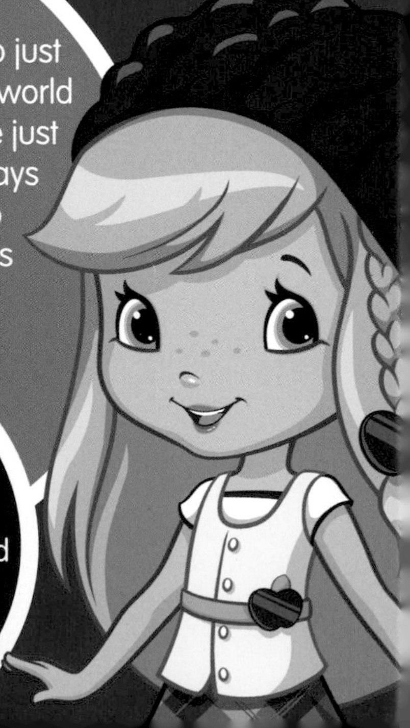

Tea Time Turtle

He is Apple's travel companion and best little bud. He may be quiet and small, but he's a great big help with anything Apple needs!

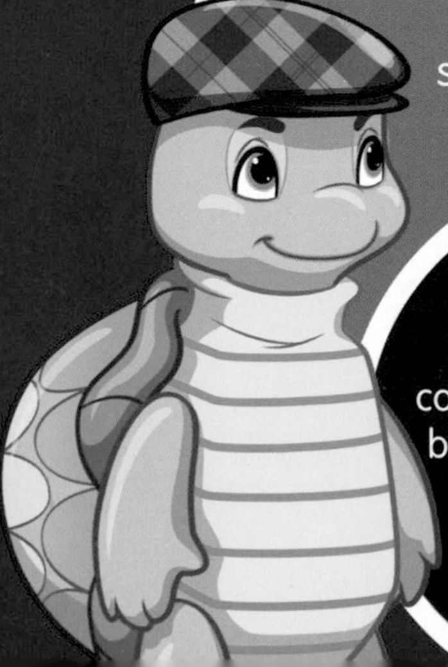

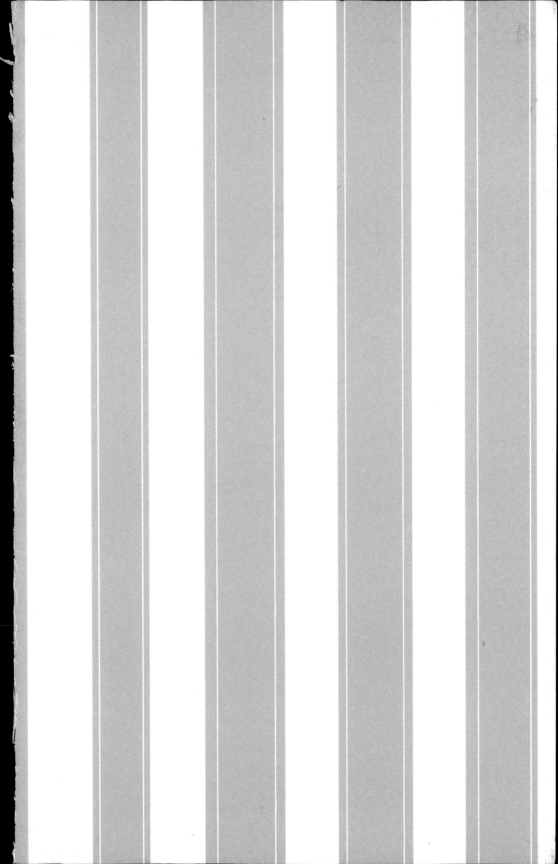

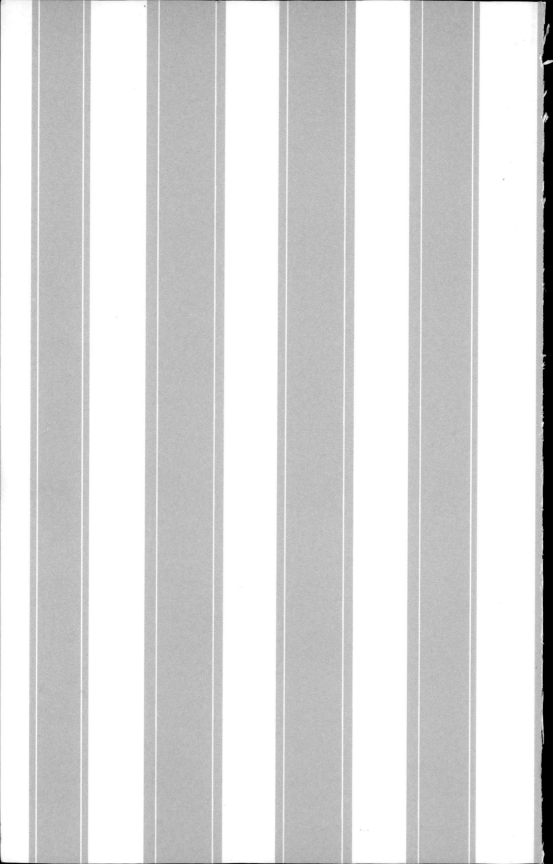